INFERNO

INFERNO

a novel

TODD RIEMER

TODDRIEMER.COM LLC

Inferno I by Todd Riemer – 1st edition

Library of Congress Control Number: 2010903660
ISBN-13: 978-0-9844827-0-2
Printed in the U.S.A.
First Edition, April 2010

Cover Art: *Inferno,* Dave Kinsey ©2010
ToddRiemer.com

For my family
living and departed

Sweet Helen, make me immortal with a kiss.
Her lips suck forth my soul: see where it flies.
Come, Helen, come, give me my soul again.

–Marlowe, *Dr. Faustus*

Part I

Wasteland

I

I dreamt myself inside a metal jar. A small space penned in on all sides by sleek iron walls. If you were looking in at me you would have seen me very small towards the bottom, pressing myself up against the cold enclosure. From outside I imagined it looked much like a vase or even a metal tin curving up at the top and coming to a fasten with a large moldy cork.

After being in the jar for some time, I reached into my ear and pulled a string of thin wire from my brain. It was a sticky substance that glowed neon blue in the darkness. I wove it into a tangled web. I pulled fine strands of memories from my ear, like a spider issuing the sap of its abdomen into the fine thread of its tapestry, its life's work. I sat alone as I knitted the faces of loved ones long dead and places destroyed. I sealed the corners with my tears and strung it from side to side in the small vessel.

Climbing up the web, I reached the top of the jar and felt the cork that closed the structure. I extended my hands, felt nail and skin slide along its rotting surface. I pushed harder and harder, believing that my body itself might transform, might, by the sheer will of my longing to be free of the darkness, the iron walls, and the world I knew inside the jar, shift from small beetle into bird.

As I threw my body into the decaying top, I felt it happen, felt my muscles moving under my flaking skin, felt myself bursting with red feathers wrapped in flame. I knew it then, as I split open the fetid lid from that rank enclosure, that I was free. I would not end my days there, nothing but dried out bones and teeth.

I awoke, still Blum. I looked down at my body. I was no bird, but rather the husk of a man nearly forty years of age. Weathered skin, blue eyes, strands of dirty hair covered my face and chin. The prison cell that had been my home for six years felt much like the jar, except a large metal grate covered the top of the ovular room. My hands, having no skill at loom or stitching, could not extract that rare and precious moistened cord from out of my brain.

There were no doors or windows except for the sealed hole above me. It often remained shut, except when the guards decided to urinate into the room. Occasionally a scrap of fat or bone was tossed down for me to feed upon. I would eat it hastily, savor each moist and gelatinous fold sliding down my throat. I sucked on the shards of bone till they disintegrated in my mouth. At times they poured water into my cell, sparse droplets I caught with my open mouth.

I thought I was inside an empty well, a cistern long drained, somewhere lost in the desert. I tried to suck the growths forming on the clammy metal walls, but they did not produce any fluid. After long bouts of silence I heard, far in the distance, high in the air, the shrill noise of cicadas and grasshoppers. I could not determine if it was the thirst or the hunger that drove me to experience the sounds, or if they were truths of the outside world. The dry sound of their legs scraping alongside each other and the flapping of their wings, sent vibrations throughout the metal drum.

I imagined myself as a locust in transition, shedding the casing of my former self to be used for medicinal properties, erotic potency, or even pumiced, churned, ground, milled into light dust to be applied to the faces of the wealthy Magistrates. To smooth the wrinkles they and I both shared.

The world of my early youth had died. It had become a history hidden by layers of ash. When the red flags began to hang from the archways of houses and wave proudly from the steeples of civic buildings and churches, when children rose from their seats to recite the anthem amongst the pitchy sound of tin drums and strings, when the trains were filled with the low faces of the Red People, mothers tightly gripping the hands of their sobbing children, when the sounds of the Fat-Bombs and the smell of sulfur on the wind became daily sensations, it was then that I knew the world would never be the same.

It had happened from the inside, an internal coup. The Magistrates orchestrated it so seamlessly, so beautifully, the coming to fruition of their intolerant Democracy. They exiled the Red People, spoke zealously of their inherently evil nature, their predisposition for deceit and treachery. It was not long before the Capital was carved apart, divided in quarters to form the Quadrants we inhabited. The walls between them were laced with wire and glass. The concrete towers that grew from them housed the Black Boots, their guns, and their ever-vigilant eyes.

The Black Boots' uniforms bore the symbol of the Democracy, three black orbs shaped into a triangle. It was pressed onto helmet, breast, and sleeve. The symbol, the coat of arms of the wretched Magistrates; I despised it. Even in my cell, in my solitude, in my unrelenting hatred for their rule, I heard the anthem ringing across the desert, the sound of the High Magistrate's rasping voice: Civility. Justice. Strength. Civility. Justice. Strength. Civility. Justice. Strength.

Only legal citizens were provided the Offering. It was delivered daily to the masses, snorted at dawn with the chiming of the bells, at noon with the high sun, at dusk with the sighting of the first star. To feel God, you must ingest God, the Magistrates proclaimed. To be God you must work as God works, unremittingly. To be saved by God you must be of the pure. The Magistrates told the people that the Offering was procured from the deity himself. They delivered it to the people, while claiming to be the mouthpiece of that invisible and omnipotent force. In years passed, I too had enjoyed the Offering, sucked it up into my nose in heaping piles. Isabelle changed me, made me see the error of my ways. The Offering was no more than the white Dust. It was shipped to the upper world from the Rogue District built deep beneath the Capital.

I also remember those who were denied God, the heathens as they were labeled, the Red People. I remember the day the trains sped away, carrying them far into the desert to the west, towards the drought-lands filled with ash, the lands where the Fat-Bombs wailed down mercilessly onto the disbelievers. Those who left were never seen again.

I sat and cried, pushed myself up against the cold metal walls to try and hear something from the outside world, but only silence persisted. I was truly alone. I thought of the last time I saw Isabelle, her once golden strands of hair covered in thick dried blood. I remembered the way she spoke of the Magistrates, their callousness, their hatred, their poisonous ways. It had been for her, my small nymphet, that I had risked it all, slammed myself against the Democracy, the hierarchy, the institution of the Magistrates. It had been for her, my Isabelle, that I had become a traitor, an enemy, a heathen. I wanted nothing more than to glut myself on her murderers' blood.

I looked down at myself as I sat in the filth. I was naked, destitute, disgusting. I was thin. I would soon be called to justice. I waited six years for the Magistrates to call me forward. Every day I felt their eyes hiding in the shadows, in the dark, watching, plotting, planning for the perfect time to undo me from my sex up towards the two lobes of my brain, as they had undone her, my beauty, my love, my Isabelle. She is no longer a woman, nothing more than bones and teeth, I thought.

I am to die, I said to the darkness.

I did not know for whom I phrased my words, the cicadas that hungrily waited to feed on my corpse, the incarnation of the darkness itself, or, better yet, the memory of the dead girl that so brilliantly existed in my mind.

I closed my eyes and imagined her with me, her warm skin, her coquettish grin lifting slightly at the corners, the way her smooth nails used to lightly scrape along the nape of my neck. If only I could scrape a knife along their wrinkled throats, I thought. I shivered with the thought of the High Magistrate gurgling and choking on his own blood. I was wet with desire to enact my own strange and wonderful experiments on the doctor who had tortured and gutted Isabelle for the expectant crowd. Those fools did nothing but look on. They were poisoned by the essence of God inside their brains.

But for one chance at revenge, I whispered to the black walls.

II

Step into the Golden Circle, the Magistrate commanded. The
unearthly scent of incense issuing from censers clung to my nose. It
gnawed at the delicate tissue lining my nostrils. Gold faces stared at
me from the shadows, expressionless faces, identical faces. The robed
men surrounded me. I paused and looked at the High Magistrate on
his throne carved from gnarled wood, accented with bones and teeth.
His red robes flowed down the sides of his massive seat in two curtains
of fabric. Rippling, folding, bending, melting curls of soft silk poured
out and collected in a pool at the base of the throne.

Your time, has it cured you of your insanity?

I did not respond. The High Magistrate's voice was deep, arrogant;
it had a quality of thousands of voices piled on top of each other.

You are a failure, Blum. To think that you could shake the strength
of the Democracy. He let out a hiss of laughter as he removed a long
brown cigarette from a golden case and placed it on a stem.

I was silent.

Blum, the time of judgment is upon you. You have two choices,
they are clear, black and white, there is nothing but one or the other. I
ask you now to repent for your sins, take of the holy Offering, redeem

yourself in the eyes of God, in the eyes of this Golden Council. I grant you this pardon, this mercy, as only I am able to give. The room was silent. Should you refuse, you will die, as she did years ago. The mouth of God speaks to you now.

He paused. I could hear tinkling bells issuing from behind the stained-glass windows, small bells, brass bells, bells that marked the long avenue leading to the Golden Council.

A dish filled with the white powder was carried over by one of the High Magistrate's acolytes. His metal sandals brushed along the rough stone with each step he took. I looked at the pile of Dust, the Offering. I had renounced the Magistrates and their Offering years ago, but it was the curse of the powder to experience, even after such long years, a longing, an intrinsic desire for the God-like bliss it provided. The dish was placed under my nose.

It is time, Blum.

The High Magistrate smirked with a sick recognition of my defeat. His brown stained teeth were half hidden by clouds of smoke. I lifted my face towards the plate and exhaled deeply so as to draw in an even larger breath. I remembered the way it once made me feel: indestructible, euphoric, seething with unspent energy. I longed for the Offering in the pit of my stomach, knowing all too well the corruption it had once bred within me, the grand trick that the Magistrates played daily with those in the streets who hailed their name in praise. As I knelt, my hands tied behind my back, the Council's eyes moving along my spine, I lurched to inhale the powder.

At the last moment, I butted my skull against the golden plate, spilling the High Magistrate's Offering onto the floor.

Fool, he screamed as he pounded the throne. You are a fool to defy me. Tell me, heathen, what is it that you desired to achieve from this act of insolence? He lit another cigarette, attached it to the stem, and inhaled. What compels you to butt yourself against the word of God? Smoke poured out from the hole in his golden mask. It covered his purple lips in long white tendrils. Three black dots formed a triangle on the mask covering his forehead and cheeks. You are surely a fool. His voice was hollow, the sound of dust spilling out of an old pipe. The censers swinging back and forth leaked the smell of dead skin, of rust, of burning sage. Well? He questioned.

My lips were dry. I spoke: The girl, Isabelle.

I thought of her face, tan skin, red fingernails, her sex issuing the scent of honey and lavender. I did it for her. I remembered the way her body shivered, her exuberant reaction when I shot the High Magistrate, permanently disfiguring his left arm. He hid his mangled arm inside of his robes. He did not desire the rest of the Council to recall the day I had brought revolution to their doorstep.

You killed her. My words trailed off, meek, exhausted, utterly desperate.

You speak of history. A decision, an action of God that occurred long ago. To this Council it is almost forgotten. He blew out another long wisp of gray smoke. The girl is no longer part of your life. You, he pointed at me, are in the here and now. It is your future we control, not the girl's. God decided her fate and it was enacted for the people, the Democracy.

She is dead. Is that not punishment enough? The spilt Offering covered the floor before me. My tears marred its delicate landscape like rain on a field of ash.

The Magistrate cocked his golden head to one side. His emotion-less mask hid his human features. He paused and then spoke: Why should I, sitting here upon the throne of God, take pity on a heathen like you? The girl is no longer your concern. She is long dead. Rather, the Democracy, the Council, those that surround you in this moment should be the subjects of your adoration, your unyielding love.

I remembered her sun-fire hair radiating outward in all directions from two sea-green eyes. I remembered her soft touch, the way she filled me with warmth, the spell she wound about my beating heart. I remembered the knife that was dragged along her full belly and the screams of her dying, as they dragged me to my cell.

I will not love the Democracy, I moaned.

Pardon? He spoke firmly. Please repeat what you have said for the whole Council so we may all hear your blasphemy.

I will not love the Democracy, I shouted.

The golden faces turned to one another as whispers filled the octagonal room. Those on the balcony leaned over to better see the face of the one who had denied the Democracy, the Magistrates, the decree of God himself.

The High Magistrate raised his arms and opened them, extended them outward to include the group of gold-leafed masks that hemmed me in on all sides. Quiet. The voices hushed. Perhaps after you have atoned for your sins in the purifying rays of the sun, after many miles of contemplation, perhaps then you may come to regret the profanity you have spoken this day. Hear you this, as you scream for God's aid and mercy, you will receive no sympathy from us. Though your eyes will undoubtedly see and crave her image in every mirage, she will no longer be yours to enjoy. Perhaps then you will come to realize the strength of the Democracy and the inanity of your ways. The time for pardoning has come to an end.

He stood up. From my vantage, sitting prostrate on the floor, he seemed immense, a sentinel cloaked in sheets of undulating blood. By defying us you have lost ownership of your actions: past, present, and future. In the heat of the sun you will surely revel in your contempt for our glorious body of command. You will undoubtedly feel pride in your insurgency. He stepped down the risers toward my slumping form. His boots made a clopping noise on the floor that echoed the beating of my heart. After all, you are the one who has injured the hand of God himself.

He stopped in front of me and leaned down towards my paling face. The candlelight reflected off his gold mask. He pulled his disfigured arm from his robe and showed me where his raw bone was exposed. He smiled at me.

It is no matter, Blum. Though I bleed now, he ran a knife along his mangled hand and let a few droplets of blood fall onto my forehead. I will heal. We will persist. It is you Blum, who will bleed in the end.

The sparkling gold-leafed audience that stretched over the balustrade roared in applause. Even if by some means you should survive and come before the Council chanting our praises, raising your hands to us, declaring us as your saviors, hear you me, there will be but one act of mercy left for you, he paused, and that will be death.

He kicked his boot into my ribs and sent me skidding across the floor. The Council roared in approval as he returned to his throne and sat down. He slammed his fist on the side of the throne to reclaim the silence. The boom ricocheted off the vaulted ceiling and the cold walls.

I wish for you to see the face of God that condemns you.

He removed his mask and stared me in the eyes, his own were two limp, gray balls set inside a sunken face pocked with carbuncles. The Magistrate laughed and inhaled from his cigarette. Swirls of smoke billowed out from his filthy mouth.

He addressed his peers: There is no room in the Democracy for insurgents. There were more murmurs from the crowd. He longs for the whore, and the only way I will deliver her to him is through a gauntlet of fire, he laughed as he released more thick gray clouds of smoke. He threw his cigarette at me.

Let this be a lesson to you all. You will all die, but to die with the promise of more after this pathetic lifetime, the guarantee of eternal paradise, that is a gift that only the Magistrates can grant. He looked me in the eyes: Those that wish for death shall receive it from us. Yet your death, he pulled his whole body forward on the throne, red fabric flowing languidly alongside his arms. It will not be quick; it will not be hastened by knives or guns. Rather, your death will be long, a journey. Take him away.

III

I was a number, one of a long string of numbers that marked my position along the chain, and I being closer to its head was #3. I was connected to the man in front of me by an iron chain attached to a large ring circling my neck. From the back of my neck a similar chain had been soldered and attached me to #4.

The guard's stick jabbed into my back. Keep movin' #3. I don't wanna see any of you lowlifes takin' your god damned time. Gunna dig the steel out of the ash. He chuckled a small belt of laughter.

My name is Blum, I whispered under my breath. He did not hear me.

Although, where you're goin' you'll have wished we could've stay'd out here longer. His breath reeked of dark liquor and I wondered if his canteen, which was just out of reach, contained water or the tart nectar of forgetfulness.

The chain was a living, breathing organism. A dozen or so men followed behind me. There were other chains, other soldiers in trucks leading other groups of prisoners, each with a chaperone of Black Boots walking beside them. The Black Boots wet their faces with water, wore military caps that kept the sun off their white skin, and ate copious amounts of fruit and nuts.

The man in front of me was massive. Each muscle, each slick, sweat-covered strand of tissue, rippled on his back. He was strong, sculpted like a statue constructed of onyx or black marble.

I watched the soldier beside me eat a ripe apple and throw the core down into the dirt. I stooped and quickly grabbed it. The guard slapped me across my neck as I swallowed the core in its entirety.

Did I say you could eat that, you treasonous piece of shit?

No, you did not, I replied frightened.

That's right, remember that you bastar'. He slurred his words, drunk.

Treasonous. I remembered with clarity how the High Magistrate's hand had burst apart, how his blood had sprayed upward and coated those surrounding him. I remembered how badly I wanted to see Isabelle after it was all done, how much I wanted to hold her hair in my hands and look into her eyes, but I had never been given the chance.

The guard walked off to the back of the line, harassed a few of the prisoners and poked at them with his polished stick.

I'm so thirsty, I muttered.

We're all thirsty, the black man in front of me replied in a deep voice. My name is Zarian.

I'm Blum, I said as my sentence was broken by a gunshot from the back of the line.

One of the Black Boots, the drunken man, fired his handgun through a prisoner's skull. The man's body fell like a stone to the ground, toppling the rest of the men bound by the chain. The metal ring around my neck tightened. A slight trickle of blood rolled down it. I watched the guard manically cut the man from the chain gang with his knife. He was no better than a butcher. He dismembered the prisoner as though he were an animal.

Jus' remember who's in charge here. He ran alongside the chain and hopped into one of the trucks ahead of us laughing to himself. The other Black Boots greeted him with victorious cries. Jus' remember we're watchin' you bastar's, he shouted back at us.

We struggled back onto our feet and continued the hellish march. After some time I looked into the distance and saw red, mud-covered faces peeking out of open windows. Their huts were small; most were connected to each other. They were covered in the loose dust. Roofs crafted from rotting burlap covered the small buildings. There was silence on the desert plains. The community, for that is what it appeared to be, was greatly deteriorated. Years of exposure to the forceful winds and the scorching sun had started to turn the mud huts into sand. Many of the outer structures were completely rotted away, the dried out husk of a corroding hive. The small faces did not leave their homes. As I made eye contact with the people, they recoiled just out of view; repositioned themselves within the shadows to spy on the passing chain of dying men.

Look, Zarian pointed, the Red People. They are mostly gone now.

His voice sounded sad, far away, I could tell he was recalling a time long forgotten. The sight of the pathetic mud-caked men had stirred a memory inside of him.

This must be one of their last settlements. He pointed over the expanse that separated us from them: Look at the way they are hiding from the Black Boots, hiding from us.

They have good reason to fear the Black Boots, I replied, recalling my own memories from long ago.

I looked closely at the face of an old man peering out from the entrance of his home. His hair was beaded and twisted into a large bundle that sat on top of his head. He was elemental, dressed in the colors of the earth. He was covered in calluses from the constant grating of sand on skin. Exile, purification, I thought to myself. The words were heavy, they bore a weight all of their own. I turned my face so that I did not have to look into the old man's eyes.

The Black Boots stopped our line. The others continued on ahead following the path of the trucks towards the dunes on the horizon. The group of guards that led us conversed. I strained my ears to listen to their words, which were muffled by the roaring wind.

It would be… teaching them a lesson. He laughed and another patted him on his back and replied: …terrible Jookie pieces of shit. You know… that they… close the route for that time.

I missed his response as a powerful gust of wind blew through my ears and distorted the sound.

Well boys… time like the present… into some fun.

The five Black Boots accompanying our line boarded the truck and drove off towards the encampment. We were left alone.

As fast as their truck sped away, our feet began to fly in the opposite direction. We ran, legs tripping over stone and pits of sand, into the vast nothing we had come from. The chain of men was uncoordinated, it moved slowly, like a jellyfish catching the pull of multiple tides at once. My heart raced violently as I ran onward. Zarian pulled me along. He did not slacken his pace. I could hardly breathe.

A man down the chain looked at me as we ran. He smiled as we hurled ourselves into the nothing of the desert. He reveled in his newfound freedom. He grinned, his eyes shined, they were wide open, until the bullet passed through his neck, carved a clean hole through his tender flesh, and continued out the other side. His body, like a sack of dry grain, hit the dust, sending an avalanche of men into the hard dirt.

I smelled fire. I distinctly remember the way the smoke smelled. It was rotten, sulfurous. It smelled like burning hide. As my body whipped around, caught inside the falling chain, I saw the red huts had been set ablaze. I saw the Black Boots dancing around as they threw large flaming bottles onto burlap roofs. I saw a soldier with a rifle aiming and firing towards our escaping chain. I heard the boom of bullets and the shrill cries of women. I tripped on the ground in front of me and hit my head on a sharp rock. My head cracked and split wide open.

Go ahead and help yourself, the dark man in the black suit said to me. The brandy is as ripe as you will ever taste. I can assure you of that.

The room was small, round, there were no doors. It was dim, lit by a small hearth and one standing candelabra. The wax of seven candles melted down its rotting brass frame. He hid himself in the shadow, just out of reach from the flickering candlelight that painted the dark walls with fading, shape-shifting figures.

Who are you? I asked. Where am I?

There was no response.

I walked over to the low round table and took a seat in one of the brown leather chairs. I poured liberally from a crystal decanter into a snifter that was provided for me.

Would you like some, I asked the mysterious voice who walked just outside the ring of light surrounding me, the chairs, and the small table.

No, I have plenty.

He lifted his hand to his hidden face and took a sip from a snifter. I looked at the candles and watched the way the wax melted, poured down the sides of the ornate brass, and covered the filigree in a soft warm layer. I took another sip and sat back in my chair, its head and arms wrapped around me. I took note of the gold studs that accented the rich leather.

Are you familiar with the rules of contract, Blum?

He knows my name, I thought to myself. Who are you? He ignored my question.

You see, Blum, I am a man of negotiation, of give and take, of reciprocity, of writing and signing contracts, pacts, decrees, statements, and the like.

He curled around the circle of light as he took another sip from his glass. His footfall did not make noise as he stepped on the stone floor. He took a seat in the chair opposite me and leaned back. I could not see the features of his face for they were hidden in shadow, but his suit was exquisite, something only a Magistrate could afford, black and white, accented with silver cufflinks and modern buttons.

You are a man of the court? I asked as I finished the burning dark liquor and set my glass down.

Help yourself to another, he coaxed as I eyed the bottle, my nerves tightening with each moment spent inside the strange, dimly-lit room. I poured another glass. You may call me your judge, although that is not my title. I have found that in the long run titles are of no importance.

Those who go to the grave with them, and those who rot without them, all turn to dust just the same. He snickered.

And what would you, my judge, like from me? I spoke from my tingling mouth.

He began: There is always a beginning, a middle, and an end. You are familiar with that, most men are.

I sat mesmerized by the sound of his voice, deep, hollow, expansive. His shadowed face absorbed the light of the candles. I smelled liquor on his wet breath. I watched the fire spearing through the wood in the hearth as I drank more brandy. He lit a cigarette and tossed the gold foil pack onto the table.

Go ahead, he offered.

I lit a cigarette while he continued; its red end glowed in the darkness of the room.

I have been watching you since birth Blum, since your beginning. My stomach began to curl up in knots. You have spoken to the darkness many times since then. I watched you for many long nights inside your cell bargaining with the air, pleading with the silence, recalling how she had once touched you, loved you, caressed you. That is, before she met such an unfortunate end, wouldn't you say Blum?

How do you know about her? I asked. Once again he ignored my question.

I have seen you dreaming of the girl, Isabelle. I perked my ears at the mentioning of her name.

How do you know Isabelle? I asked more impatiently.

He chuckled as plumes of white smoke poured out of his invisible mouth, crossed the light of the candles, and relaxed into the stillness of the room.

Blum, is it not clear to you that I know them all? Have known all that have existed and those that have yet to exist. But that is no matter, it is not how I know her, or why I know her that should be of interest to you, but rather how I may be of service to you in setting her free.

I don't understand. She is dead. What cruelty are you trying to construct for me? I shouted.

I remembered the pain I felt as the High Magistrate's doctor slid the blade across her pregnant belly. I remember the tubes sticking out of her mangled body, her delicate form, hanging limp for everyone to see. I was ashamed of her nudity, ashamed at the hordes of onlookers who did nothing to help her as she died at the hands of the Magistrates.

What is death, Blum? To me, death is but a means to another beginning, another middle, another end, he said.

You speak in riddles. Tell me what you know about Isabelle, I shouted half out of excitement and half out of fear. I leaned forward in my chair and my hands and feet started trembling from anticipation. My heart started to beat strongly. I felt the alcohol worming its way through my veins.

There is a certain kind of prison that can exist in death, my child. Your Isabelle is stuck. She is hinged between your world and entering back into the current of life. Her spirit grows weary wandering the fiery wastes between here and there.

His gloves motioned to demonstrate the separation between the two locations. My heart began to sink as he explained the truly improbable situation.

It need not be this way, Blum. She has already told me of the love you have for her.

I do, I do love her, I exclaimed.

Yes, I can see that, Blum. There is nothing to be done, nothing that can be done while her murderers still walk about up there. He pointed his gloved hand to the ceiling. Her spirit will be trapped until they are gone.

What do you need from me, my judge?

You have been wronged. That is apparent. I moved in my seat uncomfortable with his gaze issuing from unseen eyes. The Magistrates executed her. They have captured you. You have reached your end, are nearly dead yourself. Yet, there is a certain passion that keeps you from your death, Blum. No?

I was silent for a moment. The words came out slowly and left my teeth grinding in my mouth: I desire revenge.

What stands in the way of your vengeance Blum?

I don't know.

But you do know, Blum. You do, he spoke louder. It all hinges on your determination, your persistence, let us say your passion for the girl. The High Magistrate and his doctor, those that have wronged you should die. They should suffer. Is that not right?

Yes, but I don't understand, I said pathetically as I grabbed my aching head. What is it that you want from me?

There was a pause as he took a sip of brandy.

For you to denounce your mortal soul, he rumbled. Nothing more and nothing less. Such a small price to pay for the happiness you will experience while cutting the fat from their bones. Yes, Blum?

My skin turned cold in an instant. What use is that to you?

That should not be your question, Blum. Rather the question is: What use is your soul to you, when her soul suffers in the inferno? I thought of Isabelle inside a room filled with infinite flames, a room where movement forward or backward produced no result, where up ended downwards, and down ended up.

What is it that you will give me in return? I asked in disbelief.

Your life hangs in the balance, Blum. You are as good as dead. We could end things here and you could bleed out. The black man could fail in his attempt to bind your bleeding skull, or...

Or what, I interrupted.

It is not within my realm to decide when one shall die and when one shall live, that is something which fate has already determined. Yet, those whose lives hang in the balance, those whose life's thread has yet to be entirely severed, they are the souls that fall within my grasp. It would be easy to pull you down, send you towards your judgment, towards this end and the beginning of your next. But of course your precious Isabelle, she would not be there with you. She would remain suffering in the fire till justice had been served.

I must be with her, I whispered.

If you were to reach an agreement with me, I could grant you a year's time to avenge the death of the girl. That is the gift I will give to you. Do you not desire the bliss that this opportunity can create? A happiness born of revenge? Perhaps then it would be easier for you to part with such an insignificant thing as your soul?

Who are you? I asked.

The red end of his cigarette went out and the last tufts of smoke issued from his black lips. Seconds passed before he answered.

I have read your fate. You carry the potential that I once bore. He paused and then continued: But that is no matter, the choice is yours. It is simple, a soul for a soul Blum, your soul in exchange for an opportunity to save Isabelle's.

What devil are you? I asked. I was frightened of the man who spoke only in riddles.

It is of no concern who I am, the girl is your concern. She is, shall we say, on the table.

He laid out a contract on the table between us. I looked at the pages from a distance, saw the way the candlelight illuminated the black letters splayed across the worn pages. The temptation to accept his offer grew inside of my aching heart. The gravity of the decision before me weighed on my lonely soul.

It is up to you, for this will indelibly link you to the world of the dead, he whispered.

As I grabbed the papers, some ash from my cigarette landed on the document. The words were tiny, almost illegible, a small stack of old, brown papers marked with black ink. Some were singed, others flaking in places. I thought of Isabelle, her smiling face, her green eyes, the small of her back graced with a gentle sweat. I had signed before I was conscious of what I had done. The ink bled into the paper, my judge took the document back into the shadows.

It is done, he said as he leaned back into the leather chair.

Almost immediately smoke began to fill the room. I saw his sharp white teeth shining through the tendrils of gray mist. What have I done? I thought.

I must know your name, I said frantically as his image began to fade.

Like the sound of far off ocean waves, his voice rolled gently towards me: I am the Midnight Man. The smoke clouded my eyes.

⊙

I awoke in Zarian's arms. The heat from the blazing village washed up onto me.

Get up, get up you fool, Zarian shouted at me as he violently shook my body back to consciousness.

He had ripped part of his tattered shirt into a long strip and tied it around the wound on my forehead. Like the Midnight Man had promised, I did not die. I stood up, smelled the smoke issuing in great quantities from the flaming hive that just moments before had been the quiet refuge of a forgotten people. It looked like a heap of burning trash, bodies strewn randomly across the desert.

Get your stinkin' arses up you fuckin' bastar's, the drunkest of the soldiers yelled as they pulled us into a standing position.

The dead men were cut away from their restraints; their bones were left to rot on the dry earth. I imagined their spirits roaming endlessly over the barren plains, trying to find entry back into the current of life from which they came. Their bones and teeth would be the only reminder to passing travelers of their pitiable existence.

Zarian, you saved my life, I whispered to the black sculpture that moved before me. You saved my life, I repeated, shocked, reeling from the fire and the raid.

They cannot take away my humanity or compassion. You would do the same for me, he replied, quiet and yet firm.

The sound of his voice lifted into the air towards the steel quarry that could be seen scratching the horizon. Twisted metal bars stuck out of the white hills at uneven increments, breaking the line of the flat desert ahead. I could barely make them out amongst the dunes of ash and pits of dry earth.

IV

The caravan of dry wandering souls continued the march accompanied by the men dressed in black rubber boots. To think, I had once been part of them, the Black Boots. The thought that I had partaken in many of their cruel exercises in domination made me sick. I was born without a mother or father, born into the custody of the state, born into the care of the orphanage, and like the others I was conscripted at the age of eighteen.

It was not enough that the Red People were banished westward, forced to inhabit the ash lands. It was not enough for the Magistrates that they were sent in trains towards the great nothing. As Black Boots it was on our shoulders that their true fate was to rest. It was with our hands that their blood would seep into the cracked earth. It was the duty of the Black Boots to clear the Red People from the great wasteland that sprawled unchanging towards an even greater blue sky. Yet it was not until I met Isabelle that I saw the truth of my actions, the consequences of the crusade we executed upon those poor people.

Two decades before, I had walked in the same red dirt as a soldier. As I marched, I recalled Isabelle and the events of the unforgettable day we laid siege upon a settlement not unlike the one just destroyed. I remembered with clarity the insurmountable feelings that changed me from Black Boot back to man. She did it all with a look, a gaze, the green-eyed girl inside a pit of red dust altered me forever. I let myself travel back across the years, to where the smell of burnt skin rarely faded, to where I had become both murderer and traitor to the immense Democracy of the Magistrates.

All I knew was that I was one of the people making a difference, strengthening the Magistrates' hold over the world. The inside of the truck was sweltering. My uniform smelled of sweat and old liquor. A group of young men from the orphanage sat beside me as we crossed into the red desert.

The commander addressed the company, he was older than the rest of us, had scars lining his sun-blackened skin.

From my seat I listened to him shout: The Magistrates are sending us into the west. Those Jookie pigs have been plaguing us for too fucking long. You must remember men; it is our honor to clean up the country. We enable the Magistrates to do good work, to teach those heathens the power of God's command.

The commander often used derogatory language to describe the Red People, to separate the citizens from the heathens. He looked at me sternly as he downed the last of his liquor-filled canteen and lit a cigarette. I was quiet; my eyes met his. He once told me that I was among his favorite disciples. I saw the sense of accomplishment and pride in his gaze.

I remember the way my body felt at the time. Limbs forming and reforming underneath skin, strengthening, becoming something entirely different than what I had been before. No, I was no longer a boy, but rather the beginnings of a man.

We recited the national anthem, repeated the phrases the Magistrates had used to take power during the depression. Civility. Justice. Strength.

The Magistrates will create space for the new Capital, the commander said as he looked over at me in my seat. He smiled when he talked of them. The Magistrates will clear the way for progress and we will reap the rewards. No need to worry boys, there is a grand solution at play. We will have room to grow, to stretch our arms. He moved his arms outward to emphasize the great space the new Capital would fill.

In that moment I was proud, practically beaming, radiant in a way I had never been before. I looked at my commander and saw myself as part of him, saw my reflection in his face, the way he smiled, the way he moved, the way his white teeth shone in the glimmering light. I felt his heart beating as hungrily as my own. My heart was bleeding, burning, sweating. I was ready to bloom, morph, change, shed my skin like old scales, and grow to the size of a man.

The land was dry and dusty. The winds picked up tornados of sand that spun about; tops moving rapidly on the flat land.

We're almost there. You'll see it soon. He spoke rapidly, sharply. After today you will be men; today is a right of passage.

I was eager, wanted so badly to please him. It wasn't long before the fields of dry cracked earth gave way to ashy plains. It was hot. I didn't like the heat. I didn't like the way it made the backs of my knees sweat; the way beads of sweat accumulated on my neck and ran down my spine. I didn't like the way my hands clammed up, felt slick and wet.

There it was. The field of ash, so large that it ran all the way to the horizon, into the continent, into parts of the world where I had never been. Out of it sprouted small huts and houses made of mud bricks, twigs, and pieces of iron debris. There were houses attached to houses, some covered with plastic bags instead of roofs. Walls were supported by long steel girders, others held up by boxes or barrels. I had never seen anything like it. I had never seen such a place, such a city, if one were to call it that. The people were just as dry and decayed as the houses they built. The people were painted in white ash and red dirt. They looked like ghosts.

Mothers held babies in their arms, dressed in swaddling cloths crafted of burlap. Children ran free as men carried steel beams from a quarry miles away towards the city inside the ash. Women sat in silence as they braided plastic bags together. Long braids of plastic bags were used to knit blankets for their kin.

Look at those pathetic Jookies, boys.

He laughed vigorously and belched. The truck slowed down and approached the edge of a slight grade that formed a ring around the vast settlement. After taking large swallows from a second canteen, he passed it to me.

Today you are men, no longer boys. I took a large swig of the burning liquor and passed it along. The Magistrates have weeded the Red People from the Capital, but it is our job to contend with them now. It is with civility, justice, and strength that our swords will strike. He marched along the line we had formed. There will be no prisoners; there will be no one to tell the Red People's tale. There will be only the promise of tomorrow. In your minds do not forget the prospect of tomorrow, for yesterday has come and gone, born, lived, died, breathed its last breath. His voice became louder with each consecutive word. But tomorrow, he sighed, such an endless tomorrow, an infinite number of opportunities framed by sunrise and sunset. Tomorrow holds possibility.

It began so much faster than I had expected. There was no warning, no call, no whistle, or sound. The commander handed me a bottle half-filled with orange liquid. He stuffed a rag into the top of it. The people below paid no attention to us. They did not even look at us. There was no alarm to alert them of the impending danger, no bell to sound the defenses. They were a defenseless people, and in their defenselessness they were doomed.

The commander lit the end of my bottle and launched his own flaming mass into the center of a group of houses. He looked at me and I followed shortly after, obediently. The glass container left my palm, took flight, migrated like a bird over the land, and sank in a splash of crimson fire and smoke in the center of one of the composite huts.

Give me another, I shouted.

Excellent, he said as he brushed the hair from in front of my eyes and smiled, his teeth the white of polished marble.

Stupid greedy Jookies, I screamed as I hurled a second flaming bomb into the window of a house.

I said it for him, tossed the bomb so he would think me a man, but in my heart I knew that the pathetic humans before us were just men like us. The house went up in a cloud of flame, large tendrils of smoke issued from the roof, from the mouth of the door, from the bodies of the family that came screaming, horrified, out of their home. I heard them crying for us to stop. I heard them crying the names of their children. I heard them crying for God, but there was no God. There was no God for the charred ones, the Red People that ran helpless amidst the noxious plastic gas.

Flashing balls of fire fell from the sky and lit the roofs of houses. My commander laughed and continued to scream obscenities as the Red People squirmed in the confines of their huts, their connected labyrinth of shelters. I saw men dashing about with flames billowing off of their sun-worn skin. I saw roofs collapse. I saw a mother entangled in a flaming, melting plastic bag. Her child stood by screaming. Amidst the chaos, the child tried to pull the synthetic material from her burning breasts, lighting his own hands on fire.

The Capital carved itself onto the horizon many miles behind me to the east. The air smelled like an iron left too long on starched cloth. I wondered in that moment if the citizens smelled it too. I wondered if perhaps, even from that distance, they smelled burning hair mixed with the exhaust from automobiles and trains.

The commander threw a final bomb. No one from the village ran out to stop us. No one came out to fight.

They're cowards, those dirty Jookies, he screamed. They're thieving cowards. Look at them running away.

The dust covered folk scurried frantically about inside the flames.

Come on, he grabbed me, now is when you become a man.

He started to run into the village, dragging me behind him. My heart pulsed with the rhythm of the crackling fire. He jumped inside one of the first houses. The building was gutted out, but the flames had been subdued. The fire had already spread further into the center of the city of plastic and mud. Most of the people had vanished or had run in the opposite direction into the desert.

Inside the house a dead man laid on the floor, pinned to the ground by a smoldering beam. I looked into the man's open eyes as my commander ran ahead, unfazed by the chaos and the fire. The sight of the corpse mesmerized me; nothing could have kept me from staring at the man's bleeding head. I saw his tongue, pink, wiggling between his jaws as the last jolts of energy seized his lifeless body. I tried to look away but could not. I tried to hold my tears, but the smoke being as heavy as it was, dragged large droplets from my burning eyes.

It had seemed different from a distance. Inside the hut, I could not remove my eyes from the bleeding man. No. They are a disease, vermin, the refuse of society. The Magistrates' words coursed through my mind, but still I did not look away. They aren't people, they're parasites. My face was caught in a tortured pose; my nose was twisted and mucus ran from my nostrils. My limbs shuddered and moved uncontrollably as I slowly entered the back room. The sight was startling to come upon.

It's time to become a man; you're no longer a boy, he said as he held the girl down at knifepoint.

She was around my age, no older than eighteen. She had brown curls, green eyes, and a lighter shade of skin than the others. It looked as though it had been protected from the sun. It was not weathered, her hands were not calloused, her lips, plump like small wild berries, drew me in.

I looked at my commander as he took the girl. I looked at her pursed and shivering face, looked at her hands as they clawed and tore at his back. He did not stop, instead he pressed down harder into her. She dared not scream with the knife positioned so close to her windpipe. I felt nauseous, but resisted the urge to vomit.

You must become a man, he spewed out sloppily as he pressed into the girl.

The girl was beautiful, certainly a prize to be found in such a desolate hole in the earth.

Are you a man? He asked me as he looked up, sweat dripping off his eyebrows.

I couldn't move. I couldn't face him. I couldn't walk closer. I looked at the girl, her green eyes flared up at me. Her eyes spoke: I wish to die. He continued to prod her through.

The back of his head split open. I dropped the piece of wood. The girl scrambled into my arms. We coughed as I pulled her away from the burning buildings. The smoke clogged our lungs. As we ran up the slope towards the vehicle, I felt a strong tug from behind that almost sent me spilling over. I felt myself losing my grip on the screaming girl.

Traitor, he screamed at me; his body now flaming, burning from head to toe. He pulled on me as we tried to escape. She kicked him between the eyes and his body launched backwards and laid still. We entered one of the covered trucks and I turned the engine on. My compatriots continued to maraud about unaware of the treason I had committed.

I looked at the flaming village and my commander's dying body. I looked at the girl who had begun to cry.

I must go back, I whispered.

No. There is no going back, she said through tears.

Behind us large plumes of smoke stretched for miles. I am Blum, I said, breaking her fit of tears.

What is your name? Her green eyes turned to me. I pushed my

foot on the pedal. Her eyes were circles of pure jade cut and polished into two perfect spheres.

Isabelle, she said.

We were gone, racing, speeding, fugitives heading towards the Capital filled with smog, a thick layer of gray that would hide us. I thought silently as I drove: of my commander, of Isabelle, of the future I would have to bear as a murderer. Isabelle sobbed and held onto my arm.

My savior, she mumbled as we sped onward. You are my savior.

V

My eyes opened. I was dripping with sweat. Where am I? What time is it? It was night. A light ash coated everything, blown in by the winds from the north. I heard something from further down the chain. Glimmering moonlight reflected off the white ash. I saw movement and panicked. I looked around. Everyone was asleep. I saw two red eyes peering back at me, dead eyes in the night. The eyes did not blink. I heard a crunching sound and the shuffling of wet bodies.

I saw it, the bloated corpse of a man down the line from me. His head was propped up on a rock and the contents of his skull trickled down his face. Blood leaked down the crest of his forehead, ran in a steady stream down his nose, kissed his lips, and released itself from his lifeless body.

My body trembled, sent vibrations down the chain. I could not still the shaking, nor stop the sound of jangling metal. I strained my eyes to see the form that loomed over the corpse.

Oblivious to my presence, he slung himself over the legs of his victim. He had used a flat rock to flay the man's legs whose calf muscles were exposed, skinless, to the elements. Like a tanner in a leather shop he worked the skin from the muscle, the muscle from the bone, and with a ravenous, unrelenting mouth, had begun to devour the man, piece by piece.

I was sweating. I shook Zarian, lifted my finger to my lips in a pose of silence. As he woke up, I whispered under my breath: The man down the line, the man, the man, there. I pointed.

I smelled blood; it was vile. I remembered Isabelle's plump, womanly flesh. I had never desired to ingest Isabelle, to consume her in that manner, not in that macabre and twisted fashion. No, I shook the thought away.

Zarian gagged and shook his head in his hands. Suddenly, he exploded towards the thing hidden in the shadows, dragging along the men connected behind him. Zarian grabbed the demon's neck and pressed his rabid face into a puddle of ashy, bloody, water. The man gasped for air as Zarian pushed him harder and harder into the muddy ground. His panting, shrill cries woke those around us. The others circled the tangled pair. At first the grotesque display of the dead man resting limply on his bloody perch silenced the men.

After a moment they began to caw, howl, and scream into the night. They cheered and jumped, pushed Zarian onward in his determined struggle. The men frothed at the mouth, they danced, covered in a veil of white ash, ardent ghosts witnessing a battle. I tried to keep the men at bay, but they pushed and tightened the circle around the two struggling forms. I feared the Black Boots would awaken.

I looked back at Zarian. He took the chain next to the limp flayed body and wrapped it around his captured prey. The thing inhaled one last time before his body flopped into a rigid stillness. His eyes were glazed over, bugged out and swollen from the strain. He was dead. The moonlight reflected off of the flayed man's ghoulish, grinning white teeth, mud caked haphazardly on white stones. I pulled Zarian off the bloated corpse as shortened breaths exhaled from his lungs and tears streamed down his weathered face.

I heard gunshots fire into the blackness.

The Black Boots, they are coming, the men screamed.

We blindly crashed into one another, trying to escape the bullets. The cloud of smoke that issued from the Black Boots' rifles cleared as bodies started to fall beside me. I crouched to the ground, tears welled in my eyes, as the chaos ensued.

Hope you bastar's weren't thinkin' about leavin' us, one of the soldiers slurred through a mask of dark-brown liquor.

He took large pulls from an old tin bottle. As he approached the crowd that fluttered and ran, fanned about like a group of pigeons startled by a passing automobile, he shot a man pointblank in the head. I curled myself into a tighter ball as the spray of blood coated my left side. The soldier let out a howling scream as more of his compatriots came to greet us.

They began circling the group, pushing us into a tighter and tighter circle, as if at any point all of our bodies would be pushed to occupy the space of a single point. I heard the sound of weeping, of curses, the sound of boots sloshing in the bloodied ash.

That aughta teach you bastar's about escapin', another officer shouted into the crowd.

The bullets stopped. The Black Boots came in close to inspect the bodies of the men they had fired on. A few were still moving, writhing; they finished them with their handguns. I gritted my jaws tightly, felt small cracks forming in the enamel of my clenched teeth.

The officer came up close to me: Stand up, he screamed.

I stood, terrified, not knowing if he intended for me to live or die. In a blur Zarian tackled the man and I watched as he tore through his throat like a scalpel through flesh. Zarian grabbed the guard's gun and pointed it wildly at the Black Boots. The clouds of smoke, the froth of blood painting the soft ground, it had all seemed silent, slow. The moment seemed to last an eternity and I did nothing but stand still as the grisly scene continued to unfold around me. I watched as bullets struck prisoners and guards. Men stooped over to the ground bleeding from stomach wounds. My compatriots' limbs were blasted off around me. It was an executioner's carnival, yet I remained untouched. It was as if the Midnight Man's black robes hid me from the bullets.

Zarian shook me. I looked around and saw that the Black Boots were dead, as well as most of the men of the line.

It will not take long for other soldiers from other chains to find us, he said.

There was a brief moment, a gap in time crafted for us alone, in which we could escape.

Find the keys, he screamed.

Others of the line scoured the ground, many were gravely wounded. Zarian's shoulder was bleeding.

I dug through the ash around the soldier that had fallen before me. As I searched his pockets his hand gripped me tightly. It was reflexive, as if my body had decided to act by intuition and not by logic, the way I smashed the rock into the side of his head. I grabbed the key and unlocked myself as his blood cried out to me from the ground. His scream echoed my commander's from long ago. I heard his blood speaking to me as it ran down the side of his face and into the earth. I felt that somehow, somewhere, someone had seen me commit the murder. I heard the beating of his heart slowing down, coming to a close, stopping like a watch ticking its final stroke. I looked at his ballooned and swollen body before me.

My eyes swelled with tears as I ran alongside Zarian into the dunes. I ran quickly, coughing from the loose acrid dust that flew into our faces. We bolted away from the others, who would surely be found and killed. Zarian gripped his wounded shoulder tightly as we raced into the desert sands.

We ran a long distance, the ground was covered in a thick layer of ash. Small dunes formed beside us. We cast ourselves behind one of them. Were we followed? I wondered. I was exhausted. I looked at Zarian, his eyes hung low, two black circles underneath flickering hazel gems. A light dusting of ash covered our tracks. In an hour or two they would be lost. We were lost. I held my head deep in my hands. Tears poured freely from my face, down my body, and were absorbed deep into the earth, where they joined an underground source, mixed, and floated out to sea.

⊙

We had entered the ash-lands. Blasts of steam billowed out of the powdered earth. A yellow fog covered everything. The ground was littered with stagnant pools of liquid caught in sinkholes between the ashy dunes. The fluid seeped out from the water table deep beneath the desert. It tasted acrid, smelled of sulfur, burned the inside of my throat. It stung as it meandered the corridors of my insides till it poured out of me, bringing with it blood, steam, and dust. We had no choice; Zarian and I both slurped the pungent liquid, the only thing that sustained us in the brown land, the slipping landscape.

Zarian stopped and knelt down next to a pool. I watched as he washed his face. The falling white ash continually covered our skin. His hands were dry and cracked. His skin was a dark rich ebony covered in white paint, smattered with strokes of red. Every muscle and sinew of his sculpted back strained while he reached for water. I looked into the pool and saw the reflection of his face. Corpselike, his skin hung from his bones. His teeth, small jagged blades on a saw, hid behind tight lips. His lips were dry and had sores on them. They voraciously accepted the water, lips that in years passed had kissed the soft skin of women.

Have you loved before, Zarian? I whispered as I cleaned myself.

What question is that? He answered gruffly.

I looked into the pool and did not recognize my form in the mirror. Mon frère, my double, my doppelganger, my twin, my ghost, long breaths, my second self reflected back at me.

Is this what I have become? I whispered into the pool.

I have indeed loved, he said mournfully. But she has died. They have all died, memories, no longer flesh.

His words trailed off into silence. Like Zarian, my skin was split in places. I was bony, a ghost like the ghosts he recalled.

I once loved too. I still love, I said.

My fingernails were long, covered in dirt. My palms were dry and calloused, they held a fortune that I could not read, but longed to know. I turned and looked at Zarian as he washed his face and arms. He scraped the blood-stained ash from his body.

Is this the first time you have killed a man, Zarian? I asked hesitantly.

He continued washing himself. After a few moments he responded: Men do what they must to survive. His sentence trailed off. There was a familiarity, a certain sense of knowing, in what just occurred. He sounded far off, confused; his voice was that of a child's lost inside the body of a man. I have not killed before, he whispered slowly to his reflection. But my hands, he looked at his brown palms. My hands knew far too well, and then he was silent.

I thought of the man whose brain I had crushed. I took his life to save my own. I understood what Zarian meant, the reactionary quality, the knowing that comes with experience, the cool fatal delivery that only someone who has traveled that road before could possibly know. The foul water rinsed the even fouler deed from my skin.

I have murdered before, Zarian. For her, my Isabelle. He stopped drinking and looked at me.

Have you, Blum? He said.

I will again.

What do you mean?

I have made my peace with the darkness, Zarian. It is a pact that I will not share with you, something forged of blood and fate. Yet it is my intention to redeem her. It is not my expectation, but rather my intention to find her torturers and bring them to justice so that she may rest.

Is it not so that you can rest, my friend? He inquired.

No, I grabbed his hands in mine. It is not for me that I seek vengeance. It is not for my own benefit that I will spill blood. It is for her alone.

Your intention, Blum, what is your intention? He whispered to me as the dark settled around us.

It is my intention, my friend, I lowered my voice to a barely audible state, to gut the High Magistrate through.

He closed his eyes and placed his head in his hands. After a long silence, in which I watched the particles of white ash collect on his skull, he spoke: That is a dangerous road you take, though I will not stop you. He paused. The girl, Blum, tell me of your Isabelle.

I spoke to him and the darkness for hours. I began to narrate my story from the beginning, talking until my lips could no longer move. We let the ash rain down on our bodies, let the white gather on top of ourselves like a cast, until in my dreams she came to me and I lived it once again.

VI

The days after the raid were long, the weeks even longer, her silence the longest. I spent hours staring at the girl who slept day-in and day-out. We hid in the underground shed next to the orphanage where I had grown up. Isabelle and I left the truck in the outskirts of the city and migrated through the back alleys to that place I had once called home. There was nowhere else to go, no one to take us in. I could not return to the barracks for I had become a deserter.

The shed was never used, it was half buried in bracken, filled with an assortment of canned goods and old tools. I imagined they were once useful, but had been lost to years of rot and decay. The caretakers of the orphanage ignored the existence of the small compartment hidden in the overgrowth of the south lawn. It was not so much a lawn, as the grass was mostly dead. Most of the grounds had been lost to the city; a once great building had become overgrown with pipes and sewers. A once pleasant vista had become a bone yard for old tires, gears, and debris.

Inside the shed I worried constantly of the Black Boots. We hid for two weeks in secrecy before I began to believe the Black Boots presumed me dead or held captive by the Red People deep inside the desert. I imagined the headline they would have concocted for the press: *Young Soldier Murdered by Savage Desert Barbarians, Magistrates to Escalate War Effort.*

I looked over at Isabelle as I drank a small glass of water. I dressed her in a young girl's dress, the only thing I could find amongst the trash heap beside our place of hiding. The dress was old, tattered, patched with pieces of burlap and gauze. It had creases running across it, creating large ridges inside the field of white.

The thought of my commander sickened me. The thought of what had happened in the back room of that hut haunted me as I watched the dress rise and fall over her body.

In her deepest slumber I stroked her hair, touched her arm until she began to stir, moved myself close enough into her space so that I could smell her scent, the odor of her body, which coated her skin in a thick and glorious sap. It was divine, it was something entirely different and new, something I yearned so much to be a part of. If she were the sea and I a sailor, I would have cast myself into the body of her waters never to return. She stirred.

Her face turned up towards mine. My smile met her vacant gaze.

Have they all died? She asked.

Have who died?

The people, my village, she whispered. I did not know what to say to the girl.

Yes, I suppose. I was gentle, for she was fragile. I imagined my words touching her on the way out, spilling over her in a way that only a man can. Was that your family, Isabelle? Were they there inside the village? She was a ghost. She did not respond.

I looked at her skin. It was a rare coat inside a world of black and steam. Isabelle, I said quietly after some time had passed and she turned over to rest again. How come your skin is lighter, compared to the others of your people? A few moments passed as I listened to her steady breathing. Have you always lived with the Red People? Are you from the desert?

Her voice was hollow, sound spilling from a glass jar. Blum, it is a miracle that I have survived as long as I have. My people are a dying race, a lost civilization. Soon enough they will be completely gone. Their history is lost, it is forgotten, as mine is too. I do not remember much before the desert. The time I spent inside the Capital's Red Quadrant was short and I was young. My father was a citizen and my mother, Red. They broke my family apart when we were exiled. I have not seen my father since.

She became quiet for a moment and I could hear the passing of automobiles on the streets nearby.

We were labeled so many things, Blum: heathens, criminals, vermin, demons. When we arrived in the dust, many of the older men were killed on site, others shipped away to work in the steel quarry. Women and children were forced to live in shantytowns. We built them from the desert wreckage, the remains of a world long destroyed. It was only a matter of time before they wanted all of us gone, eradicated, purified. The last word caught in her throat, had stimulated buried emotions.

The Magistrates are bent on our removal. We are gone from the Capital, nearly gone from the desert. She sounded empty, lost, speaking from the innermost corridors of her brain, her primal and fearful self.

Something terrible happens when one human being supposes himself better than another, claims to have found the light when others are lost, reached the highest pinnacle when others have remained low. Something terrible has happened and it will go on until they are stopped, her voice faltered, or we will be forgotten.

I am here for you, Isabelle. There is nothing the Magistrates or the Black Boots can do to take you away from me. Our fate is one. Can't you see that? I said as I moved closer to her on the small broken-down cot. Our fate is now tied together. We will be exiles together. I touched her arm as I laid next to her, and though I wanted badly to take her then and there, I did not, I withheld my desire, my passions, my intrusive and instinctual masculine proclivity to breed.

Blum, I don't think you understand. The Magistrates have nearly succeeded. There is nothing we can do now. They are too powerful. There will be no record of our existence; no memory but the memory I keep inside.

She moved my hands so that they wrapped around her. I could sense the beating of her heart, I felt it quickening, doubling over with each second like my own.

No, I interrupted as I sat up.

What? She replied.

You are not forgotten. You are not yet gone. They may try and change the story of what has happened, but can we ever really forget the truth? The Magistrates may rewrite the past as they like inside their archives. That is all an illusion. The Magistrates cannot rewrite what is in here. I moved my hand over her forehead. Or what is in here. I moved my hand over her left breast. I felt the smallest of my fingers gently grace the crest of her nipple and she shuddered with my touch.

I stood up and turned away from her as she sat up on the bed, her dress slipping off her right shoulder. The Magistrates preach otherwise but I know that there are other ways to the center, to God. The way is inconceivable, it is not calculable, or finite. I turned to look at her. Try as they might, and they have succeeded with many, I will never accept them as the gods they claim to be.

But are you not a Black Boot? She whispered.

No longer. I replied.

And the Offering, how will you exist without your precious Offering? Many have tried, but most fail in their attempt to wean themselves off the Dust.

It had already been three days since I finished my supply of Dust. Though I had gone against them, deserted my commander as he died, I could not control the compulsive urge I felt to snort the remainder of my supply. I no longer imagined it as the body of God entering me. I was disgusted with myself, but I could not resist its power.

I have found something more important to me than that. There is no going back. I am through. I looked down.

You have strong willpower, Blum. That is admirable. She looked away from me. Though I will tell you now, it is not for me that you should stop. If you truly oppose the Democracy, you will cease for yourself, for your freedom, your own future. Do not put all of your faith in one that no longer has a future.

I have found you for a reason, Isabelle. I said.

She looked back at me. I took the small band that circled my left bicep and ripped it off my worn uniform. The piece of red fabric fell to the floor, the crest of three black dots looked up at me from the ground.

I do not have the answers to fix this world, to solve all of man's problems. I do not pretend to have the knowledge to guide you either.

Yet, I will try my best to ensure your future. I paused and came over to the bed to sit once more and took her soft hand in mine.

It is through your own life's quest, your struggle to fulfill your own happiness, your own instinctual need to find meaning with all of this, I lifted my hands and moved them to encompass the small room, that the answers exist. And, like all things, they are inexplicably unique to each of us. I leaned in to her ear and whispered: And I, I have found my answer in you.

I did not understand the laws of courtship, but perhaps it was my innocence, the naïveté that only the truly fresh and untouched have, which won her as my prize. It was a small place, a place where the memory of my childhood loomed, but it was an escape from the Capital, the anthem, the lines of Black Boots that marched the avenues. I did not crave the Dust, but rather, Isabelle. It was peaceful in the shed. The tombstones of machines and pipes sat heavy on the brown earth above us. I heard the sound of bells ringing from the steeple of a stone church.

She turned to me, her face was smooth like cream, like sand, like polished bones coughed up by the rough sea. Her eyes were two green, glass discs.

You are so naïve, Blum, she said as her slight smile slipped and fell away.

I did not care what the nymph had uttered to me in the thick moment. I knew that she had felt it, even if for just a moment, the raw energy that exuded from every single one of my glands, exuded and wove my pheromones into an inescapable net.

I watched the way her hands fiddled in front of her white dress. It was too young for her. It made her look premature, undeveloped.

It flattened down her breasts in an awkward way that stimulated my intrigue with the girl. I watched her hands grace the tops of her thighs, watched her fingers gently pass over the fabric that hid her sex, watched her nails scratch her small bony wrist. She looked away. Strawberry lips, the natural scent of jasmine, it was as if God had rolled her in the sweetness of a young girl.

I wanted so badly to touch her lips to mine, spread them apart, and place my tongue on hers. I moved my hand to hold hers. Her palms were delicate; her skin was soft. Mine were rough and sweaty. I was nervous and she was quiet. I longed to lick her skin, taste the salt of her body. She leaned in closer to me and whispered in my ear.

I do not believe in God, Blum.

She put her hands around my waist and brought me into her dress. My body started to shake, my nerves were fragile, delicate like antique glass. She moved her hands over my pants, moved her fingers across my buttocks, and gently squeezed. My throat, my tongue, my gums salivated for hers.

I did not know how to please a woman. I had not yet discovered the ecstasy of feminine curves or the smell of hair coated in rich honey-eyed perfume. I had not yet seen from on top, makeup lining white lids, or pearl earrings dangling back and forth from soft lobes, or lines forming on fragile hands as they dug their way into my back. I had not yet experienced that kind of pressure exuded on my naked form. She paused as her sodden breath wet the hairs on my neck and I felt my sex fill up with dark blood. She looked me in the eyes and as they met mine I felt an electric current pass between us.

She pulled me into her and spoke: I have lost my faith in men,

Blum. Men make mistakes, men are fickle, men are corruptible, men die. My mother learned this all too well. She once spoke of times before the coup. She told me stories of empires from long ago. Tales of countries and cities now turned to dust. She knew mythologies of other Gods, other worlds, other beliefs. My mother was gifted; she tried to teach others about the stories, the histories as she called them.

What happened? I asked her as my lips quivered and my sex found the space between her thighs.

She looked at me, no longer smiling: It was men that burned her at the stake.

My body gave way to her more experienced hands. I felt my skin melt with her touch. My intestines churned with desire. My heart pumped loudly. I was sure she could hear it. She bit my lips as our tongues met on the inside of each other. She lifted her dress so I could see all of her. My eyes met the dark corners of her private self. I touched her thighs, her hips, and dragged myself on top of her. I did not know how, but instinct led me through her. I feasted on her body; I drank and ate of her. I tasted her inside and out. She tasted like honey, like cantaloupe, like salt water. She winced as I stretched myself through her. My heart raced as sweat dripped down my brow onto her flat stomach. I thought, as we smashed ourselves into one being, as the pressure built inside of me, that surely both of us would combust into rich strands of scarlet flame.

As she slept, I reveled in her remains, soaked myself in the memory of her touch.

Isabelle.

The name rolled off my tongue. The taste of her still coated the roof of my mouth, my lips, most of all coated my white teeth that were spread wide open, dozens of white pearls grinning.

VII

The gray dust fell from the sky as we marched sullenly into the wastes. Blasts of air worked into every crevice of my sweating skin. It licked and tongued my ribs, ran between my thighs. I thought of Isabelle and the way her hands had discovered my most intimate places.

The land will swallow us, Blum, Zarian shouted while covering his face with his hands as the dry wind pelted him with falling ash. I walked behind Zarian, hiding from the biting, whipping winds.

We must find shelter, I screamed, but my voice was lost under the song of the dunes, lost underneath the layers of filth that rained from black swollen clouds.

We had begun our great migration back to the east, back to where the Capital hunkered inside a gloomy valley, where a thick shade had permanently fallen over the vast steaming metropolis.

We must find shelter, I screamed, once again fighting to make myself heard over the currents of air.

There is an outcropping, Zarian shouted towards me. There is a place, though it is not large, he said pointing to a grouping of gray rocks, half covered in ash. The rocks broke the flurries of dust and the howling storm enough so Zarian and I could huddle protected behind them. I held onto Zarian as the winds continued to whip up the ash and rage about the ruins of the great desert.

Zarian spoke under the tempest into my ear: How are we going to make it back to the Capital? It will be a miracle if we survive this place.

I was distracted. I combed the past thinking of Isabelle.

She left me. She left me in the bunker during the night. I said aloud.

What, the girl? Your Isabelle, why? What happened to her? He said.

I don't know. I can't comprehend, even to this day, what it was that drove her from me. Perhaps it was the weight of her past that drove her out into the cold city alone.

I brushed the ash the best I could from my face. I was thirsty.

Perhaps she did not want to impart her memories to me. She did not want to be responsible for the fate that she would inevitably bring upon us both if she had stayed.

Three gusts broke the clouds above us and for a second through the veil of white I saw the dark sky and the moon's light above the clouds. The next grouping of clouds washed away its gentle glow.

It was as if she knew her fate would crush me.

And the Black Boots, he whispered, did they not find you hiding?

No, it was as if I had slipped from their memory, the actions of my crime had been forgotten, never traced back to me as its source. My name, my life before the raid, had all but vanished, and I was lost to the Magistrates and the Black Boots, a name written in a register undoubtedly marked deceased. I was Blum and yet not the Black Boot I had once been. No one cared of my fate or the fate of Isabelle. She just vanished.

Vanished? Zarian whispered, puzzled. But you saw her again, no?

I ducked my head under the rocks as more ash wafted over its crest.

There were many dark years, my friend. I paused. When I found her again, she was different, had taken a different form, morphed. Though, underneath her costumed exterior, she was still the girl I had met, had tasted and enjoyed.

☺

It had been five years since I had seen her, my Isabelle. Those days were long gone. When she left me I broke down. The world was meaningless, despicable. I failed to wash myself, feed myself, dress myself. I became a denizen of the streets. I would not have survived the cold winter months if I had remained a vagrant.

Finding work became my only option. They did not require names at the steel mills, only able bodies, and although I was a shell of a man, I still retained the muscle needed to build the Magistrates' machines. After a few months men change. I adapted to survive. Though I wanted to die, I lived on.

Yes, I gave up my convictions, worked for the Magistrates instead of against them. But what reason was there to fight? My Isabelle was gone. I lived alone in a small flat. It had one window that looked down on a small crowded street. It was often too cold to open the window.

During the nighttime I thought of Isabelle. I had forsaken the Offering for her. Though it was delivered weekly to my door in small packages, I dumped it into the sink. I could not break my promise to Isabelle. Rather, the memory of her had become my addiction, the center of my longing.

I sketched her in my private journal, fixated on her eyes, the way the small lines of her irises composed a perfect blend of green. I decided that if I was ever given the opportunity again, I would take her away from the city of steam and steel. I would keep her for myself and no one else.

Mostly I recalled her sweet taste and smell. I wrote words of how she felt. I listed her in adjectives and nouns: peach-like, feathers, orange peel, olive oil, soft stone. I kept my journal a secret, although I do not think anyone else would have been interested with what was written inside of it.

When I was alone, I thought of her as I enjoyed myself. I dreamt of her enjoying me just the same. I hallucinated the small dress she had worn. I elaborated on her visage: I dressed her in white stockings, in high heels, in red lip stick, in blush, in flowing gowns, and undressed her till she was starkly nude.

In the desperation of my loneliness I shouted her name, believing that if I yelled it enough times she might hear me and, by some other-worldly force, materialize. I often felt her eyes on me while I dreamt. I opened my eyes, half expecting to see her delicate, tender body close to mine, but she was nowhere to be found.

☉

I could not sleep. I got up and put my clothes on. It was the middle of the night. I need a drink, I thought. I lit a cigarette and walked down the street towards the bar. The neon lights drew me in. The room was dingy. The must of old liquor and sweat was everywhere. The scent of vomit was apparent with each step into that dark hole. The lamps hung low, burned and flickered, covered the silent, twisted figures searching for intoxication in dim light.

I took a seat on a leather stool cracked from overuse. Yellow eyes peered at me from every corner. The liquor burned its way down my esophagus, flowed through my heart, arteries, and veins. My liver and kidneys pumped the poison through and out. I was a machine. My eyes, blurred by brown liquor, scanned the room feverishly. My cigarette burned and long curls, tendrils of smoke, covered my face. The smell of it entered my fingers, dug into my nails.

Through the smoke I saw the decorated face of a whore in the night. Her cigarette cast a ruby glow on her cracked and dried skin. Her hair, matted, slightly damp, was black. Black dye covered gray hairs. Her eyes were lined black; her irises shot darting looks from side to side. Her perfume wafted towards me through the scent of old men and booze.

She gave her body to me. It was old and used, but the feeling, the need, the compulsion to want to be part of someone else drove me forward. The need for me to understand her from the inside, know her crevices and her smells, the way her skin folded, consumed me. The desire to feel her breasts, her hair, her fingers, clawing, gnawing, biting into me, the necessity for me to feel the pain grew. I imagined Isabelle pressed tightly to my chest, her nails digging lines into my back. Hot gusts of breath entwined us and we became one.

Isabelle, I cried out a number of times.

The whore did not react; she did not care. I was certain that many others who had come before had called her far worse names.

As I discovered her body, nothing like the woman I had once enjoyed, I noticed the way her skin hung loose around me. It was like paper, so thin you could almost see the blood running inside the spider veins that shot up and down her thighs. Her buttocks were old, flabby, they did not crest into two voluptuous parcels of meat for me to enjoy, to eat, to savor the flavor of her. No, she was pitted. My hands ran down her backside as I climaxed.

As I took another look at her sleeping figure, I threw the dollars onto the bed. No feeling, no emotion, nothing but the stench and the sweat, the stickiness and the fatigue. Her form was small and shriveled. I hunkered down over her face, her intensely dark face, her painted face. I saw the hues of makeup she wore in swirling patterns. I saw the cracks that lined her lips, the wrinkles that marred her eyelids, her flaking scalp and her graying hair, the paint now flaking in areas once covered. She was flaking away, the face of a corpse decaying in a tomb, the painted face of a whore in the night.

As I walked the barren street back to my flat, it started to rain. Fog rolled into the streets and steam issued from underground storm drains. The lights and fires of the city flickered under a black sky pinpointed with light, like the needles of an acupuncturist sticking out of a great black face. Big drops fell and washed the foul stench from the city. The gas-lamps flickered in the downpour.

I looked across the narrow street and saw a woman dressed in a fur coat. The cap on her head held feathers and ornamental beads glinting in the moonlight. Her hair was short, curled, bobbed in at her neck, black. She looked at me briefly before dashing into a nightclub. I have seen those eyes before, I said to myself. There was something familiar, strange about them. My heart raced. I followed the woman inside.

The lounge was quaint, dark, quiet. A host grabbed my jacket and hung it up on a hook with the others.

Thank you, I said.

He did not remark. He was a lifeless gray face, one of the many that dwelled in the city. A low rhythm filled the smoky room. I lit a cigarette and continued inside. People walked about, exchanged glances, a few held low conversations. It was not wise to speak loudly in public. The Black Boots that marched the streets day and night were everywhere. They were stationed every few blocks on street corners, in classrooms, in factories, in public plazas.

A waitress came over to me: Can I get you a drink, sir?

Velvet, on the rocks.

Thank you, sir. She wiped off the table and scurried away to get my drink.

I watched the fur coated woman: Is that Isabelle? I questioned myself.

Waitress, I shouted. She came back over.

Yes, sir?

Is that lady alone? I asked her.

Yes, sir. She just came in.

Thank you. Would you send a bottle of Spark over to her? Your best bottle.

The waitress pushed off to get the bottle I could not afford. Isabelle, I remembered the way the name filled me with longing. The waitress brought the bottle over to her, pointed at me, and explained the situation to the woman with the ornamental hat. She looked over; a small smirk overtook her face. Her green eyes glowed in the faint light. I walked over to her.

May I have a seat? I asked.

Certainly, she replied, a smile on her slick, pink lips.

The waitress filled our glasses and placed the bottle in a bucket of ice. It sounded like nails on a chalkboard as it slid into its frosted home.

What business do you partake in, here in the Capital, Mr.?

She paused waiting for me to fill in the rest of my name as she took a small sip of Spark, a drag from her cigarette. The liquid bubbled in the glass, small beads of air traveled through the intoxicating fluid. Her soft lips parted, drained a small mouthful of the crisp nectar and placed her glass back down on the table with an inquisitive smile.

Well? She said.

I took a sip to settle my nerves. I did not want to tell her I had become a machinist. I did not want her to know that the boy from years ago, who rescued her, the same boy who once spoke of protecting her future, had once again become a part of the Magistrates' bureaucracy.

A persona unlike my true self, someone confident, sexual, someone with an ambition and power that I on the inside lacked, spoke through me.

Mr. Lewis, I replied.

She must recall the time we spent inside the shed, I thought excitedly.

I'm a bureaucrat for the Senate. I work in the Crate District on the north side of the Capital.

The lies flowed out of me, landed in her ears, traversed the lobes of her brain, and I could tell, as her eyebrows perked up, that she was impressed with my cool and calm demeanor. My persona lit a fire within myself so strong that for a moment, I could not even remember who I really was.

Excuse my attire, I said, I never wear my suits in the rain. Luckily my black shirt hid the oil stains and the rain had done a good job making everyone appear as disheveled as I felt.

The Senate? She said. What do you specialize in, what is your forte?

She laughed a schoolgirl's laugh. Her laugh featured the white teeth I had once licked in the shed.

Oriental Policy, I said. I looked around to make sure that no one heard me. It would be unwise to be caught posing as a bureaucrat. I continued: And you, what is your name, your profession? It slid off my tongue, fluid and calm, a sense of bravado exuded from my chest.

I was waiting for it, the name I had repeated to myself millions of times, a name I would and could never forget, Isabelle. My eyes were wide open waiting for the word to come forward, my pupils dilated as the seconds passed, the pleasure of her memory filled my pants. I had scrawled her name on hundreds of newspapers, books, and journals over the years and here it was, come home to greet me again.

My name is Mina, she said.

The name struck me upside the head, left me breathless. I recoiled at first, shocked, and then my face smoothed over as I decided to play her game. Does she not recall me the way I recall her? Is she not the girl, Isabelle, with green eyes like sea-glass sparkling in the sun? Is there not a head of golden-brown hair hidden underneath that cropped black wig? I drank more Spark.

I am a social woman. Mostly parties, openings, plays, but to tell you the truth the theater bores me now. There isn't anything worth seeing anymore.

By that statement I knew what she meant. The arts that glorified the Magistrates' campaigns were celebrated, the rest were burned.

She continued: Don't worry, Mr. Lewis. I'm not married.

She laughed again, and I wanted her. I wanted to taste her lips again and knew in that moment that I needed to possess them at whatever price.

I'm surprised I haven't seen you around the Capital, she remarked, drinking the last of her glass of Spark and pouring us another. Tell me sir, have you been to the Orient? She put out her cigarette butt. The smoke curled up in long wisps. Have you seen the jungles, the tigers, the savages? She laughed that same schoolgirl laugh of innocence.

No, it is no longer permitted, I said.

She looked down at her watch, a dainty silver piece, curved woven mesh, beautiful, sparkling. It accompanied the beautiful silver ring that ran on her finger like mercury molded to her bones.

Well, I must be going, she said.

Wait, already? I replied, shocked she was leaving so abruptly.

I have a prior engagement to attend.

It is so late though, how does a young woman like you manage to travel around the city, with such, um, I paused searching my brain for the right word, confidence? Certainly not by yourself, I presume?

No, Mr. Lewis. She smirked. I often delight in the company of men, that is, for a price. She stared me in the eyes as she got up and straightened her hair and her coat. Are you going to come with me? She asked me pointblank.

I would like that very much, I said choking on my words. Her lips looked soft, like velvet or satin, or even the way moss appears when it is damp, covered by the shade of a tree. I motioned the waitress for the check. We left.

We walked down the street. I did not hold her hand, but I contemplated it. Each time I almost grabbed her soft skin my stomach turned.

The party is just around here, she said as she pointed down a long dark alley.

Down there? I questioned.

Yes, there is a pass through at the end.

One more smile from the girl alleviated my uncertainty. We started down the alley, it was damp, her heels made a splashing sound as they traipsed through the water. I thought to myself, this girl, this is the same brave girl from years ago, I am sure of it. I could not see; it was quite dark. I did not see a pass through or passageway.

She grabbed me and thrust me up against the wall. If you struggle I'll castrate you so fast you wont have rocks to fondle, pig. She slammed me into the trashcans inside the narrow alley. Just because I'm a woman doesn't mean I won't stab you through, like I've done to all the others. I felt the tip of her knife caress the top of my retreating sex. I felt her strong grasp cutting the oxygen off from my brain.

Now tell me, Mr. Lewis, who is supplying the Magistrates' Offering? She slackened her grip a little.

I don't know? I said genuinely, while coughing in short dry bursts.

Don't lie to me. Someone of your status should know and I'm not afraid to pry it out of you. I felt the knife pierce my clothing. Don't play with me. I'll stab you right through. She lifted the knife and put it up to my neck. Speak, pig. She spat on my face as she clutched me by the neck and held me at knifepoint against the wall. I enjoyed her red fingernails on my neck.

Wait, wait, I gasped, barely able to breathe. She lightened her grasp so I could speak. I don't work for the Magistrates or the Black Boots, Isabelle. I missed the sound of her true name. Isabelle, it resounded in my ears.

She gasped. How do you know my name? Who are you? She belted as she pushed me against the wall. I watched a pair of rats scurry out from the piles of trash behind her. I saw them pass her black high heels. In my mind I had imagined her in red.

Blum, Blum. I spoke quickly. I was frightened and yet oddly aroused. I am no bureaucrat.

She let go of me and stepped back. The knife still waved before her face. She looked stunned, her face melted into tears. She dropped the knife to her side.

Blum? She looked at me with new eyes.

Why did you go, Isabelle? Why did you leave me? I loved you.

You thought you loved me, Blum. When you have walked these streets there is nothing but fucks and money. There's no more love, Blum. She spat out the words, desperate.

I approached her; she did not back away. I grabbed her wrists and she let the knife fall. I embraced her. Through shortened breaths she spoke: Even you, Blum, fucked me. I'm not the same girl, Blum. You are not the same boy. You look older, different, changed, broken.

We're all broken, I said.

But I've found someone to take me away from all of this, Blum. I've found someone who is going to change everything, something worth fighting for.

Who, who is going to take you away? I said concerned, looking once again into her shimmering eyes.

The Saint. We are going to take them all out. Take them down once and for all.

She was panting and I felt her breasts on my chest. Like a ragdoll she crumpled into my arms and fainted. I carried her through the back alleys to a cheap hostel, paid the fat, sweating manager in coin, and dragged her through the foul smelling hallway into a bedroom.

Inside the room I laid her out on the stained sheets. I saw the way her breasts almost fell out of her black dress. I did not touch her, though I wanted to. I saw bruises on her arms, marks on her wrists. What happened to my nymph? I asked myself. I watched her for hours as she slept. I recalled myself as a young man watching her in the shed beside the orphanage of my youth.

When she stirred I handed her the hot water.

Thank you, she said.

When did this happen? Why did you start this, I paused, profession?

She looked around at the squalid room; a brown stain ran across the ceiling. I offered her a cigarette and lit it, the smoke twisted in front of her face.

Girls like me have two choices, go to the factory and sew uniforms for the Black Boots, or fuck 'em dry. I live off the one thing they want from us. I let them have me until I get every piece of information I need from them. Then they are dead. I have killed dozens.

Isabelle had become something dangerous, a pool of gasoline near an open flame. The seconds next to her were exhilarating. I sat there waiting for her to explode.

I won't let anything happen to you again. You'll be safe now.

I don't need you, Blum. I left years ago to protect you. You were better off without me. Mine is a life cursed by death. I found the Saint and he has showed me a new way. She took a large drag, crossed one leg over the other. I have him now. He is going to bring a revolution, you'll see.

    I'd like to, I said.

    She looked at me.

    Then come with me tomorrow night.

VIII

When the storm passed, Zarian and I found ourselves inside a valley of dunes. The remnants of houses could be seen littering the expanse. Crystalline trees bloomed haphazardly from the rotting soil. A thick layer of ash coated them. The trees smelled waxy, like formaldehyde, a mortuary, embalming fluid. They were fragile. One issued a thick sap that drained about its base. It was red, viscous, pulled slowly towards the earth by gravity, by magnetism, by weight. Sap drizzled out of it like saliva had from Isabelle's seething mouth. I recalled it with great clarity, a mouth foaming with red frothy bubbles, spouting incantations as she clung to the last vestiges of her life.

What happened here? What happened to the homes that once stood in this part of the world? I asked Zarian who passed me a handful of the roots he had uncovered from beneath the ash. The roots were rich with water, they pulled the liquid from deep inside the earth.

The Fat-Bombs, Blum.

He passed his hand over the bark of one of the brittle trees and snapped off a small twig with ease. He held it to the sun, watched the way the rays of light divided as they passed effortlessly through the nearly transparent foliage.

It looks like glass, he murmured.

The crunching sound of his feet over the crystalline ground sounded like hooves, like the growing and fading clop of draught horses before the plow.

He spoke: They tested their bombs here years ago. It was before the Capital had become what it is today. It was a time when scattered villages still existed, before the Great Consolidation, the forming of the Quadrants, before the Red People were all but gone. He looked at me. I lived in a town like this once, long ago, before the war.

I have not seen much of the world outside of the Capital, until now, I said.

Most haven't. Zarian replied. He crouched to the ground and put his head in his hands. I once lived in a town like this one, he repeated, softer and slower, more drawn out, his voice a waterway clogged with the pollution of his memory. I was lucky to have left before the attacks. I remember seeing the bombs falling on faraway settlements, on the heathens as they were marched out into the desert. I remember the explosions; thousands of shards of clear glass ricocheting off of man, woman, and child. Whole communities were demolished; small cities became studded in broken glass. Splinters of shattered glass stretched for miles around the epicenters. Huge craters filled with nothing but glass and sand, and ash. The ash rained down in heaping piles. He stood up and looked out over the distance, I looked too.

Looking eastward towards the center of the valley I saw towers, very far away, poking out of the sand and slipping earth. I remembered the Capital that I had been banished from. I remembered it all: the fountains, bridges, electric lights, carriages, blasts of steam bursting from underground trains. I recalled the sound of phonographs filling the air between hulking gray and copper buildings, occupying the space between canyons filled with smoke and light, calling the masses to the factories, calling them to take their daily Offering, spinning the loud anthem across the city streets. Beyond the dunes, beyond the broken crystal trees, it stood, lonely, waiting for my return.

They all had names, Zarian said as he walked on.

Who, Zarian? I whispered.

The people in the ash, he muttered. Look. He pointed to a group of statues, casts made from hot ash and glass, which stood amongst the dunes. From my distance they radiated like white marble. They were beautiful. Three women still as milk in a glass, still as the polished bones that they resembled, white like paper, white like cotton, white like teeth. I looked intently, my vision blurred by the sun.

They still have names, he said as we approached the figures.

Each woman was caught in a final posture before the explosion, before being encapsulated. I reached out to touch one of the figures. Zarian pulled my hand back.

Do not invoke the dead, he whispered. They have suffered enough. Do not make a mockery of their final pose.

I'm sorry, Zarian. I didn't mean to disturb them.

My family is dead. They are amongst the casts of people that remain, where everything else has fallen away. He paused. Not here, not these.

After a moment I spoke: Do you wish to tell me about them?

No, he said despondently.

I looked at the woman in the middle. She was middle-aged, robust. I knew that someone must have loved her, before the Fat-Bombs, the ash, the smoke, the Magistrates' great dream of purification. I desired to know her and touch her once smooth skin, her once fair hair. I desired to hear her soothing voice, have her small hands touch me with tenderness, a certain sensuality that only the small hands of women and beautiful nymphs contain.

I desired her, my Isabelle trapped inside the ash. I longed for her legs, fair and hairless, her plump hips upon my thighs, her moistened mouth agape, ready to inhale me, swallow me whole, capture me, lick the sweat from my brow, enjoy the darker parts of me that in the moment were limp. I had once powerfully held her, powerfully delved into her sex.

No, it is not her, I said as I repealed the thought.

I looked deep into the eyes of the woman before me. They were two holes, black and sunken in. She looked at me and I heard Isabelle calling my name.

Blum, your Isabelle, how did she pass on? Zarian asked.

Memory unhinged itself like a knot untying in my brain, unfurled itself like the Magistrates' wretched flag.

As usual the meeting was long. The crowd was quiet and listened to every word he spoke. Something seethed underneath the surface of his tan skin as he orated. He was patriotic to an extreme. He breathed revolution, a return to the way things were before the Magistrates had monopolized the word of God. He used rhetoric to light fires inside us and fanned the flames with a hatred so pure, so true, so instinctual, that it brought blood to the surface of his skin. His capillaries swelled under the hot lights. Large beads of sweat rolled down his perfectly angled nose, fell down onto the metal podium.

His speech was intoxicating. He delivered pun after clever pun, landed metaphor, and simile. He used inflection to bring his voice to a crescendo and pulled out with an energy equally as magnetic, leaving us to fill the gap in emotion with our cries. I wanted to be him. I wanted to speak those words myself, but knew that on the inside I could not, would not allow myself to. The power of those eyes ever moving on my body fastened me to my chair.

I wanted to ingest him. In times past I had read of such a condition, where a subject is driven to eat living organisms in order to collect and then exude that creature's spirit energy. A belief in that type of animism would certainly be considered foolish and heretical by the Magistrates. I did not care. On the inside I could not be contained. My thoughts cycled and circled about, a vortex of wild fantasies and desires.

I sat there listening to him as he finished his speech. I was utterly enthralled with the way he moved his fist up and down with each deadly shout of prose: ... and so it is that the Magistrates have taken from us our voice, our possibility, our choice. It is not news to you, who have suffered under them for too long, that they have taken away all reason, logic, and thought. Strength in uniformity, strength in purity, strength in order... but at what cost? Who are we as humans without those characteristics that separate us from the savage animals? What are we without our individuality, our idiosyncrasies, the passions that make us unique? The Magistrates would have you believe that it is for your own protection that their laws, their rules, their Black Boots exist. His voice reached a pinnacle, it was higher, faster, more fluid, and seethed with rage. He paused.

The underground room, lit by neon light, was filled with a circle of fifty men and women who crowded and huddled together. He hunkered over the podium and moved his gaze from person to person.

What is this war? What purity comes from murder? What civility, justice, and strength is there in the sacrifice of those who have no means to protect themselves? He shouted: War is but an agenda of the wealthy to occupy the time, energy, and thought of the poor so that they should not rise in revolution.

I suppose I was to blame, as we all were, for a small part of the Magistrates' success and growth, their inertia as they moved across the globe. There had been no choice but to follow their law or to accept death, I thought.

Lift your tired frames, weathered eyes, and broken bones. He continued. Lift one foot and place it before the next. His fists hammered down and his hair dripped with sweat. Deny the Offering, not to punish those that have punished us, but to let that newly freed and furious soul of yours dictate a future filled and fueled by passion, reason, and free will. It shall be so, he shouted, like a train moving at full speed down freshly slicked tracks.

Join me in revolution, join me in the act of overthrowing…an automobile zoomed overhead washing out the next few words… me in an act of creation, liberation, and let your burdened soul, which is now wrapped up in a tight twine by the Magistrates' claws, light a fire so thick and smoldering that it combusts. We will start a conflagration of the mind so powerful that the very ocean itself will smoke and steam, washing away order to pave the way for a new world.

He stopped, exhausted, sweating, panting. His torso fell onto the lectern. He was utterly spent. I wanted at that moment to take his heart and eat it, feed from the energy that coursed through his veins and arteries.

I could tell that he fascinated Isabelle, that he inspired her, that he made her desire, made her lust, satisfied her need for revenge. I had become a regular. I was fascinated by the way Isabelle dripped over him, used him, delighted in his body, sucked on and enjoyed each and every confident word that spilled from his mouth. She stood behind him in the shadows. I knew that I could not do those things for her in the same way that he could, but still I would try.

Isabelle and I looked at each other over his shoulder. The girl knew the power she held over me. It was no secret I cared deeply for her. Something that had been rooted in history had sprouted into a flower inside of my guts. Most people came to the secret sermons to vent, to expose their problems, to be part of a greater whole, to express their concern in an otherwise unconcerned world. I, on the other hand, came for the girl.

I watched her take him by the arm and lead him into the back room through the red sparkling curtain that draped across the small stage. I stood amid the sound of cheers, thinking only of the man and the girl. Then, with new confidence, delivered to me by some unknown source, I followed them into their hidden quarters.

I interrupted them. He had removed his coat, his shirt, his pants, and was sprawled out on top of his makeshift bed. She was next to him, nude, half covered, grinning at me. Her lips parted ever so slightly so that I could see her white teeth.

Hello, Blum, she said.

Isabelle, I whispered.

Come in, Blum, St. Ignatius said invitingly. What is it that brings you?

St. Ignatius, I wish to serve you further. I have invited the men you told me to conscript. I have charted the activities of the Black Boots for weeks. I believe in what you say. Is there something greater; is there something more I can do?

I had only attended his weekly sermons for a few months, but had quickly cemented myself as a supporter of the cause, the revolution. St. Ignatius took note of my never-ending desire to please him. Contrary to what he thought, I didn't do it for him, but rather for Isabelle.

He sat up and exposed his body to me like a young man exposes himself to his first lover. I did not shy away from looking at his naked form. It was too beautiful to look away from, sun-stained muscles rippling over solid bones.

Yes son, the time for revolution is upon us. I have been watching you since you arrived some months ago. A good find, Isabelle. It is clear to me that your passion for the Magistrates' demise is strong. Shall I tell him? He looked at her and smiled.

She nodded.

Isabelle requires a special task of you. She is in need of someone of your, talent. He looked at me, analyzed me from top to bottom. I could not discern his intention, though his gaze was erotic and powerful.

I looked over at Isabelle, watched the way she massaged her calf muscle, taunted me with her form, while he stroked her hair, unaware, or indifferent to my apparent lust for her. I linked my hands together and scratched at my palms.

Come sit.

He motioned for me to sit next to them on the bed. I sat down trying my best not to reach my hand out and touch her leg.

Our Isabelle has decided to make a journey, Blum. You must accompany her. There is cause for me to believe that we are close to the apex, close to the pinnacle, the great change is upon us. St. Ignatius always spoke as if he was presenting for a large crowd, as if his voice was being heard by millions.

What is it that you desire of me, Isabelle? I asked her, curious as to what bureaucrat, soldier, or Lesser Magistrate she had to seduce in order to retrieve the information that had incited her call to action.

Isabelle was an artist and the body was her palette. She used it far and wide over the Capital, and like a black widow often it was only her who emerged from the web she had so cunningly drawn her prey into.

Isabelle got up and poured glasses of red wine for the three of us, her naked form only inches away from me. My pupils widened, my stomach filled with an insatiable hunger. She tied a sheer wrap around her breasts and torso. It was delicate, nearly transparent. St. Ignatius did not mind that she exposed herself to me. I wondered if she had told him of our lovemaking, of the time I had saved her from dishonor and death.

It happened two nights ago, she began. There was a man, she looked down, and though she retained her smile I imagined that on the inside it harmed her the way she had to open herself to the dark men of the world. I secretly hoped that like the others she had used for her own purposes, perhaps she had been doing the same with St. Ignatius, that somehow her coupling with him was only a means to an end.

He told me of the Magistrates' source for the Offering. The Dust they feed the people, to tighten their hold on the citizens.

Every mentioning of the Offering made my stomach tighten. Though it had been years since I had consumed the powder as a Black Boot, the hunger for it had never completely left me.

There is a place, she looked at us both in a serious way. There is a place, she repeated, deep under the city, the Rogue District, where the demimonde rule. The Magistrates allow it to exist for one purpose and one purpose only, the bargain they have struck with its ruler. Shipments of Dust are delivered and distributed weekly to the citizens from that underworld.

She waited to continue as a stream of traffic passed by overhead. We have found a way inside his world, we have found a passage into the Rogue District. We must learn what we can of the Magistrates' plans before it is too late. She crossed her legs tightly over her sex. Maybe then we can understand the key to their unraveling. Maybe then, her voice faltered, we can break free.

St. Ignatius spoke: I have seen what lies beneath, and though I have spoken to Isabelle about what exists there, I cannot convince her otherwise. I traversed the grounds many years ago. It is dangerous and though I may serve to lead you in, I may not be able to lead you back. He looked at Isabelle as the two of them shared a silent exchange.

No one spoke as we stared at each other. Destabilizing the government, the Black Boots, and ending the purification of the world, that is what Isabelle desired above all else.

She continued: The source of the Dust will lead to the source of their power. To control the Dust will be to control them. The High

Magistrate will fall. Order will be lost.

She smiled. I looked at the girl and thought that perhaps by God's compassion, if we might be able to survive the deeds to come, perhaps then she might love me.

St. Ignatius stood up. I stood as well, a new heat rising inside of me as Isabelle approached us. St. Ignatius put his finger up to her lips, sensually, desirously.

A toast, he said. We raised our glasses. To the revolution, he said with a grin.

He pulled Isabelle so close to us I could almost feel her breath on me. He looked into my shameless, starving eyes, and sensed that I needed her. I drank a large sip of the purple wine. It stained my teeth the color of crushed blueberries.

We shall cement our new pact, he continued, as he pulled her into his nude form and kissed her lips generously, strongly, with a sense of confidence that turned my nervous core to soft down. He bit down on her bottom lip and pulled at it, a piece of skin caught between diamond jaws. His masculinity was intoxicating. I could smell the cigarettes he smoked and the cologne he wore. It was not repulsive but rather robust, masculine, powerful.

I followed suit and kissed Isabelle. The three of us fell, bodies entwined onto one bed. I pulled the black wig off her head so I could see her hair. It draped about her nude shoulders, my Isabelle's perfectly tan, fleshy shoulders.

That night we listened to the music of the streets, laughed, and ate of each other, made plans through strokes and gestures, expressed visions through groans, and fulfilled fantasies that would be acceptable in the new world, the new order that we would bring with the coming of a new sun.

IX

Take my hand, she said. She reached outward and I clasped onto her glimmering wrist.

St. Ignatius had adorned her from head to toe in the most expensive pieces from his collection. Although he spent most of his time inside the secret den, under the speeding trains and marching troops, St. Ignatius had accrued a wealth unmatched by most of those who did not belong to the Magistrate caste.

The years of donations and secret heirlooms left in the revolution's name had become, with time, his own personal bounty of exquisite garments, old world rarities, and antique jewels. In exchange for offering his churchgoers a feeling of freedom, they in turn took good care of the man who claimed to want nothing more than the eve of anarchy upon the footsteps of the Magistrates' door.

I held Isabelle's hand as we stepped out of the automobile and into the darkness. I followed her into the covered alley that led deep into the catacombs of the lower sections of the Capital. There are places in the world that one rarely desires to remember. Yet, it is those particularly malevolent spots that seem to hibernate inside our inner minds. Like a festering sore they grow inside of one's psyche, blossoming at times, though undesired, and spread themselves like a thick rotting blackness over even our most wonderful of recollections.

Underneath the city, the Magistrates' laws did not prevail. The people of the Rogue District ran a world fueled by hedonistic desire. It was a world of the flesh, where young girls could be bought for pennies, the law was built from breast and loin, and even one's most sinister wishes, most disturbing and disgusting fantasies, could be brought to life with coin. The Rogue District, although dangerous, excited me, and though I had heard of it in stories, I had not yet been privy to its secrets.

We reached the end of the dark alley. The streets were silent, the moon covered in cloud, the rains would come soon. She held tightly onto my hand. I enjoyed the way she gripped it with her freshly painted red fingernails. St. Ignatius had layered her in a heap of pearls and silver. Her eyes lined richly in thick black paint, her face veiled with black sheer mesh. She would be an offering to the people of the night, but we would be there to guide her, chaperone her through the darkness.

St. Ignatius grabbed the iron ring and banged the large black door in three solid strokes. A small round hole opened in the door. A man looked through the opening and examined us.

Exactly who do you think you are? He stated with an arrogance that did not match his unsightly visage.

St. Ignatius spoke: We have come with business of our own. I bear the symbol. Let us pass. He lifted a small medallion out of his shirt. The Magistrates' crest of three circles forming a triangle was embedded inside a silver ring.

I listened.

Those that bear the mark are permitted beyond the door, but tell me sir, he said suspiciously, who is the girl under the veil?

She is a gift. We have brought her as an offering, something to persuade *him* of our loyalty. St. Ignatius bowed slightly, not removing his gaze from the gatekeeper. I wondered who the man was we were to meet at the end of the dark road.

Open the door, St. Ignatius commanded.

The small circular hole slammed shut and in a moment the great black door opened, revealing a long spiraling staircase. I continued to hold Isabelle's hand as we passed through the entrance. The small man was no longer in view, he had already become one with the shadow, had left us as quickly as he had greeted us.

The scene at the foot of the stairs was not too dissimilar from the alley we had walked to enter the district. It was dark, our footsteps shuffled over pieces of garbage and pools of water. I wondered if the rank liquid bothered Isabelle. I wondered if in time she might let me wash the dirt from her heels, allow me the pleasure of cleaning her tired soles, worn toes, small nails, and perfectly shaped arches.

Where did you acquire a Magistrate crest? I asked St. Ignatius.

Our lady acquired it the other night. He smirked as he looked back at Isabelle.

We walked through the barren, dark alleys, the places where the corners had yellow eyes, where shut doors led to underground bars, whorehouses, and chemist laboratories. She was afraid. Her hand trembled in mine as I grasped it. I would not let anything happen to her. There were no lights. I could not tell the height of the ceiling, as it was hidden high above us in the darkness. There was a quiet I had not expected, a solitude I did not like. No, I will not let her go, I thought to myself.

St. Ignatius had warned us of the dangers of the Rogue District. It was a place where there were no rules, a place where you might end up dead.

The Magistrates allow this to exist? I whispered to my companions.

She spoke: They have no choice, Blum. There are some places in the world where even the law cannot extend its reach. There are some places not worth conquering. This is one of them. Her voice was barely audible. There are two worlds, one underneath and one above. I do not imagine that anyone from down here could overtake what they hold up there. She looked suspiciously at the shadows that moved around us.

St. Ignatius spoke: The Magistrates have free reign over this place. They allow the people of the night to live here because they pose no threat to the Magistrates' power. In their harmlessness they are protected. That is why we have been granted access, why the shadows keep themselves at bay.

I looked around and I could barely make out the figures in the windows of broken down and crumbling buildings, but they were there.

They know we come bearing gifts for their leader, they know we are protected by the Magistrates' crest.

The veil, I thought. I wondered if it somehow designated Isabelle for their taking. I dreaded the exchange that might occur, and for a moment desired to turn back, but I did not. Through the darkness, I saw the eyes of the dead looking at me. They peered out from dark holes in brick walls and from broken windows of abandoned warehouses.

I would not look so closely, St. Ignatius whispered as he put his hand on my shoulder.

How did it get like this? It is as if an old city was destroyed and then another city was built on top.

St. Ignatius pointed at the buildings around us. Yes, Blum. The wars of older times are chronicled here. Some people were forgotten, or perhaps not forgotten, left behind.

We continued onward, circling the sunken avenues of that quiet graveyard of a city. Some lampposts still remained on street corners, though none were lit with the fire of the upper world from which we had come. Most passageways were blocked off with concrete slabs, or large rocks that had fallen from above. It was an expansive cave, lined with old steel girders, the remains of a dead civilization.

Have you been here before? I asked the Saint. His knowledge of the place was more expansive than he had led me to believe.

Many years ago, Blum. That is a past I do not wish to live again. I have crossed over. I am no longer a part of this world of the damned.

I looked at Isabelle but she did not look back up at me. I wondered to myself of his intentions. If he knew of this place before, why had he waited till she had discovered it herself to take action? Why had he not tried to put an end to this before?

I don't understand, St. Ignatius. How is it that you lived in this place?

After a few moments he spoke: I have nothing to hide from the two of you. Isabelle did not look at him. I was once lost. Abandoned as a youth, I had to find my own way to survive. During the nights I placed myself in front of burlesque houses filled with Black Boots and rich businessmen of the city, who during the night fancied something different than their wives who were waiting at home.

He spoke as if he recalled it all with great clarity, as if his past was not as hidden as I had thought. When he began to speak again his words rushed outward, a waterfall of memories.

That is exactly where I stepped in. Hello good sir, hello generous sir, hello, hello, hello; I sang to them, wooed them, showed them just enough to make them interested. They were drunk fools. I pulled up the fringe of my fur lined coat and strutted before them: I see you are interested in business tonight, I see that you do not have an attendant for your meeting this fine evening; adieu, adieu, adieu. I danced for them, Blum.

Most walked away uninterested. Most hung their heads low, drunk and low. Yet, in the group there was always someone whose curiosity outweighed his reason, or even someone who had tasted of me before. You see, given enough time, and all I had was time, one could learn to master any art, any seduction.

I would bend them: Well I am glad good sir that you have let me join you. Where is the meeting this evening? What kind of advice do you need? How best can I offer you a consultation? I spouted like a tape set to play over and over again. I shot them a smile, a grin, and charming dimples. I raised my hands in reaction to what they were saying, laughed aloud, and with grace gently slid my fingers across the nape of their neck, a faint skimming, like a spider walking across a pond to fetch a fly, and then retreated back to the comfort of my pocket.

Isabelle did not seem uncomfortable with his story, and neither was I. In the darkness of the underworld it seemed normal, reasonable, something that even I myself could imagine being tangled up in. I dismissed the thought.

He continued: My actions must not be confused with love. There was no love in those consultations, rather that was sport for coin, something the darkness and solitude had taught me well. It was a means to an end.

I see, I replied. How did you manage to break free of this place?

That is a story I do not wish to relive, Blum. A pause. Shh, listen, he said. We approach.

It was quiet at first, then came the sounds. We continued to follow the music through dark alley and street, followed it into the furthest stretches of the black city. Quite suddenly the neon world unfurled before us, a cacophony of shouts, songs, and screams swirled around. Fluorescent light painted me purple, red, and green.

A woman covered in snake tattoos performed a public flagellation on a man chained to a brick wall. I saw girls in windows sucking honey off of other girls, laughing, giggling. I saw prostitutes and gigolos, young boys for sale dressed in feather, face paint, and leather. I saw business men dressed in black cloaks, their faces covered in gold or silver masks, hiding their identity, creating a veil of doubleness that I was beginning to succumb to myself.

I saw animals too: there were small parrots of many colors trained to fly through flaming hoops, monkeys in wooden cages hanging from wires, and small white crabs racing around as gamblers threw coins on the floor in hopes of striking fortune. I looked to my left as I maneuvered through the plaza and saw a man repeatedly lighting himself on fire, but he did not burn. My mind raced, my pulse quickened, we had reached the Rogue District.

The place smelled of a thick sulfurous smoke, there was a certain freedom, a certain wildness and bohemian spirit that made me feel energized, liberated, and finally, after years of suppression, allowed me to be truly unbound.

I was a blind man soaking up sensation with a large sponge, free finally to drink of the pure ecstasy of hedonism. I drank of that world liberally and mercilessly. I drank to glut myself. I drank to no longer feel the fetters that held me down.

Amidst the chaos, I did not see him at first, but I smelled him. I smelled the cologne he doused his half naked body in, rippling indigo in the flooding and flashing firelight. I smelled him, muscle and bone. When I turned around, and peered out of the dark alley, I laid eyes on him for the first time.

He is here, St. Ignatius said.

Who? I asked.

Jex, the master of this world of the night. Follow me. He grabbed both our hands and walked through the crowd approaching the man reeking of oils and smoke.

Jex held himself with an arrogance that attracted me, made me momentarily desire him. Isabelle looked at him in the same fashion, looked at him desirously, though when I saw her gaze upon his musculature I knew inside she desired nothing but a path to vengeance. My fascination with the man quickly turned to suspicion and jealousy.

Most stared at him, as though the people of the plaza regarded him divine. They parted around him as if unworthy to be graced by his presence. I caught another waft of his scent, his uninhibited masculinity: rust, bark, and sweat. He moved as though he had experienced all before, with a pride demanding the utmost respect, while exuding the least amount of reverence for those around him. They loved him the same for it, fell to his feet as though he were a god.

Jex poked throughout the crowd, flirtatiously grabbed and pulled those that he desired, whether man or woman, into his firm grasp. When he leaned to kiss them, it accentuated his soft warm tongue, the way the stubble grew on his chin, and the cut proportions of his angled faced. His jaw was strong, his body firm. I studied him, as did the girl, and the Saint that stood beside me.

Jex's smile spread in the flickering lights. A ravenous smile that only the purely malevolent truly master. He revealed his teeth, two rows of perfectly polished white river rocks inside a mouth of flesh and gum. His pure blue eyes gazed over at us. He smiled as he recognized St. Ignatius. I felt my bones shiver with contempt for the bargain we were about to strike.

Come with me, Ignatius, Jex said as he grabbed Isabelle's hand and moved back through the crowds towards a building across the way. I followed behind, praying to God that inside she loathed him as much as I did.

X

The crack of a gunshot broke my storytelling and sent Zarian and I diving into the piles of ash beside the crystalline women. It was hard to determine if the noise had come from far away or from nearby as the sounds inside that place resonated between the glass trees and the sparkling dunes.

Are they close? Zarian whispered to me from behind a small hillock.

I had leapt in the opposite direction taking shelter behind a similar mound amongst the glass-studded trees. The sound of voices filled the expansive landscape. The gray dust and ash distorted the approaching voices to an unintelligible level.

I looked over at Zarian, across the expanse that separated us. In a panic he began to bury himself in the dust, coated his black body in the powder that had once been old homes, skulls, and meat. The voices were getting louder. I did not bury myself, rather I crawled through the ash, belly to the ground, like a snake slithering in the sand, towards a farther dune.

The voices were nearly upon us. I thought it had come, the moment of my death. I thought the Midnight Man had decided to drag me by my heels back into that room of stone and smoke. Suddenly, the dune I repositioned myself beside slipped and broke like a crashing wave on top of my prostrate form. I was encapsulated in the ash, like the women I had seen before. I was covered, could hardly breathe, and yet dared not move.

Look there, an escaped prisoner. The gruff and angry voice of a Black Boot soldier bellowed into the ash.

I was quiet. My body shook in anticipation of death. My heart-beat rang inside my bones like a clock ticking its final seconds before it stops. I fully expected the skeletal hand of death to pull me out of the pile of ash.

I wouldn't move if I were you, a second soldier spoke.

I could not see them, the ash covered my eyes, painted me as white as a ghost. Isabelle, I imagined her soft hands covering my mouth, pressing my lips together in an unbreakable seal of silence.

Get up from there, the first voice commanded.

I heard a scuffle. Zarian moaned in pain as he was dragged to his feet.

If you move, we will kill you.

Zarian did not speak. I prayed he would not reveal my location. My brother, mon frère, my darker twin; my eyes watered as the dust continued to pour about me. Small pieces of polished glass stuck to my skin in dozens of places. Once more I heard the gun explode into the sky. Zarian screamed out of fear. I gritted my teeth.

Is there no one else who goes beside you, heathen? Do not force us to make you speak.

No, he whispered. His voice was muddled inside the wind. There is no one.

I heard the struggle of bodies as Zarian grunted.

You will pay for your treason, prisoner. I heard the soldier spit.

I would kill them all again if given the chance, Zarian screamed out at the soldier.

A crunching sound. Zarian coughed heavily. I imagined him doubled over, blood dripping profusely from a cracked nose or broken rib. I imagined his chapped lips tasting the metallic essence of his body as it dropped onto the white canvas ground, staining the land with his blood.

The pain you caused our comrades will be doubly inflicted upon you. The Magistrates do not look kindly upon treason. The way you have so defiantly braced yourself against our authority will be punished. Follow us now, prisoner. Come.

The crunching sound of boots on crumbling earth vibrated through the ground.

No. It ends here.

You will obey me. The other guard yelled.

I will never obey you. Come, take me winds, I heard Zarian scream into the sky. It would not be the first or the last time you have taken an innocent man to his grave.

I will finish you quickly if you redeem yourself in the eyes of the Democracy, the first Black Boot said. Tell us you love the Democracy, heathen. Tell us and we will end your pain quickly.

I would rather die a hundred deaths, I heard him cry into the wind.

I did not move. There was nothing I could do.

Enough, the second Black Boot shouted.

The sound that followed was gut wrenching. At first it was only a muffled scream, but then came a long groan that brought Zarian's body to the ground.

The first soldier spoke again: Tell me you love the Democracy, maggot. Tell me you desire nothing more than the mercy of death.

Zarian spoke slowly: The Democracy will fall. The Black Boots will fall. Kill them for the girl, and for me, Blum.

I cringed at the mention of my name.

The first: Who is it that you speak of? There was no response.

The second: Leave him to his slow death. Come. Let us go. We will tell the Magistrates of this Blum.

I hid inside the ash dune until I could no longer hear their steps. When I rolled out from my place of hiding, Zarian had been covered in a layer of falling ash. His blood leaked mercilessly around him. I cradled Zarian's dying body in my arms. I scraped ash from his frothing and fuming mouth. Night had begun to fall. My arms were covered in his blood.

Fool, I whispered. You're a fool. I am cursed. I said as I exhaled deeply and rocked him like a newborn babe. What have you done? I stuttered on my words. His pulse was barely there, he did not respond. I choked on my tears as I wiped the ash out of his eyes and mouth. I pawed at his skin, his face, swept the white chalk from his nose. Don't leave me here to die alone, I said in desperation while rocking his cold body. Warm tears landed on my cheek. Why must you die? I screamed into his silent face as I batted the ash from his form.

I felt the Midnight Man's eyes upon Zarian, peering at him from the shadows ready to seize his soul. Zarian's blood washed over my sun-parched skin. His fate was sealed. I looked out towards the distance, towards the great city that sparkled with neon and firelight.

I will avenge you, I said to the dead man while gazing blankly at the towers. The spires of the Capital poked out of the white land. I looked at Zarian's dying eyes and I recalled her own.

☉

Jex opened the wooden door to the main chamber. It was dim. The room was draped in fabric. It swung from one side to the other in long flowing sheets that cascaded down to the floor. The curtains were decorated with ornamental beads. The sheets of red and purple drapery reflected the gaslights that lit the way.

We passed private alcoves filled with pillows. Large glass pipes, burners, and lanterns barely illuminated the shadows. Some alcoves were occupied. Some were empty. The few people who lurked about looked at us mysteriously as we passed. Some of the women were topless, their breasts exposed to the smoke that swirled around them. Their nipples were adorned with jewels and paint. The men that sat next to the women were dressed in black suits. Some of them wore masks to hide their faces. They groped their escorts, played with their exposed bodies, licked and caressed their bare skin.

The smell of Orange-Labyrinth was extremely heavy; cleaning fluid, orange zest, pine needles. The smoke issuing out of the water pipes and other baubles created halos of orange around the flaming lamps. I felt the smooth cool of the Orange-Labyrinth smoke filling my lungs. I felt like I was floating. The colors of the fabrics were more vibrant. The sounds of low chatter, giggles, grunts, and chimes were heightened. In that state, I felt my gnawing desire for the Dust grow stronger, as if one substance had summoned my craving for the other.

Jex led us into to the main room. Do you want anything to make you more comfortable, perhaps a drink? He motioned for us to sit on pillows surrounding a low circular bronze table. Isabelle sat between Jex and St. Ignatius.

I have something special for you, he said to St. Ignatius as he brought out the syringe and a few glasses of dark liquor.

I don't need the Drips anymore, he motioned for Jex to put the syringe away and Jex complied. Jex handed me a small glass of liquor.

Cheers, he said as we raised and clinked our glasses together.

I downed the liquid in three gulps. He took a sip of his and set his glass down. The dark liquor mixed with the fading buzz of the Orange-Labyrinth. It brought out my unconscious desires for the Dust even more.

What brings you down here, Ignatius? Are you returning to me? Jex smiled a wry smile, a malevolent smile, a smile that told me much of the thoughts in his mind, the thrill that power gave him.

Better yet, Jex, he spoke up.

He took Isabelle's veil and removed it to uncover her beautiful face. Jealousy shot through my bones as Jex inspected the girl. He looked at her manicured nails, the way her breasts sat on her chest, the mountain of charms St. Ignatius had ornamented her with.

Ah, I see. The girl is a divine specimen. She is quite remarkable. He turned to look at me. The young man, what of him? He asked St. Ignatius. I was shocked, for I had until that point considered myself only an escort to St. Ignatius and Isabelle.

The young man, he replied cooly.

St. Ignatius looked at me and I could tell in his eyes that he was not surprised. He thought for a moment. The silence ate at my brain.

He spoke: I am willing to part with them both for the right price.

Jex thought momentarily. They can stay. I will give you forty percent. That is the agreement I am willing to make.

It happened quickly; Jex's concubines surrounded Isabelle and me, lifted us both to our feet. They clothed me in a white linen robe, though they left the girl in her black ceremonial attire. I did not struggle. Jex momentarily retreated to the back room.

St. Ignatius, what's going on? I asked him under my breath.

You wanted access to the source and I have brought you this far, he replied.

I looked at Isabelle. Did you know about this?

She looked at me: I did. Do not be afraid. I will be here with you.

Her voice calmed my nerves. However, I did not trust the way in which the arrangement had been crafted. I did not trust the eager manner in which St. Ignatius sold us into servitude.

I must return to the surface. St. Ignatius spoke to the girl and me. You must understand, it is with love that I do this. He turned around. I will see you before the end, my disciples.

St. Ignatius, I shouted after him. St. Ignatius, but he did not look back. I tried stepping towards him but two dark men moved out from the shadows of the curtains to stop me.

Isabelle came up behind me and whispered in my ear. Don't worry, Blum. I am here. Her voice relaxed me. I need your protection, Blum. I need your strength if we are to stay in this underworld. I turned around just as Jex returned and motioned for us to sit down. He circled my body, pinched my muscles, ran his hands across Isabelle's firm buttocks. My insides churned with every touch and prod of his hands on our bodies.

How long have you been working the streets up there? He asked me as he removed the syringe with the amber colored syrup from his pocket.

Years. I lied.

And you? He addressed Isabelle.

I am no streetwalker; my clients are from the highest castes. I am an escort, a courtesan, and you will be surprised with the skills and talents I bring you.

I did not recognize the side of Isabelle she put on display for the man that drew closer to her. Even her voice had a different inflection; it was seductive and dripped out of her mouth like honey.

We shall see, he said to her with a smile.

My eyes were fixed on the syringe that filled up as he pulled back on the plunger. The two of you have come to me for what reason? Why have you decided to leave Ignatius, or as you call him, St. Ignatius? He chuckled, making fun of the way we had elevated his name to such an imperial status.

He tied a tight band around his arm and delicately placed the needle into one of his large blue veins. I did not answer his question but watched him. His eyes opened wide, exposed two rings of white around his irises. His body jolted upward, stiffened as he felt the full effects of the chemical orgasm. Afterwards his muscles released, putty-like, and he fell into a state of quiet relaxation.

Isabelle spoke: I found Blum some time ago. She motioned toward me. He is my attendant. St. Ignatius took us in, provided us with care. He told me of your world. She looked around and motioned to all the fineries around us. I have heard of your power, Jex. I knew it would only be a matter of time before we met, joined our strengths into one.

The word *one* sent an electric feeling through my gut.

He looked at her and doted on each word that she uttered, as did I. Her language massaged his ego, delicately touched his masculinity from top to bottom. She leaned into his face. Her act was quite convincing, however I hoped that her words were only that, an act. Jex had fallen under her spell, the web of desire she wound tightly around his heart had been set in place. Jealousy burned inside of me.

I look forward to reaping the rewards of this friendship, Isabelle. There is no doubt that your talents will bring much fortune to my house. Yet for now, he turned to look at me, my appetite demands someone of a different nature. Give me your arm, Blum. He commanded.

No, I won't, I spoke to him.

You will, Blum. You are mine now.

I looked at Isabelle as Jex wet a cloth with the remaining drops of alcohol in my glass. He cleaned off the needle, tied the cord around my left arm, and rubbed the alcohol over my bulging vein. He bit down on the tie to tighten it and make my veins protrude. My veins looked like little rivers traveling down my forearm. The veins continued down my arm, got smaller and smaller until they sprouted into my fingertips. Isabelle looked away; I could tell she could not bear to watch the act unfold.

I gritted my teeth angrily as the needle penetrated me. A slight pinch and then, as if a bomb had exploded in the room, my eyes widened and filled with a myriad of colors: orange, pink, green, blue. The colors swirled and mixed before me as my heart began to race, my genitals began to tingle, and then as if a thousand stars burst forth before me, a brilliant white light filled my vision, and I heard nothing but the sound of static.

My mind floated somewhere between heaven and earth. I played with the colorful melting fabrics that surrounded me. I spilled myself into the pillows and molded them in my fingers like rich clay. I shouted words that took the forms of animals: ostriches, panthers, gold fish. All the while the smell of Orange-Labyrinth filled my nostrils like a shower of tangerines coming down on top of me.

Time passed and Isabelle and Jex had transformed a million times before my eyes. It was somewhere in that moment that I felt him. As I looked at Jex he appeared different than before. He was faceless, dark, shadowed in the undulating blackness. Suddenly, I felt him inside of me. I felt him wanting to know me inside and out. I felt his essence rippling through my blood, as if a swarm of flies had found their way inside my heart and coursed through my veins. As suns and stars spun in orbit above us, I saw his white teeth smiling at me. I could not move. Where was Isabelle? I tried to speak but couldn't. I was filled with dread as the dark creature's parts ran through me, and then there was only blackness.

I awoke in the early morning; the den stank of fluids, of alcohol, of stale smoke. Jex laid sprawled naked on the pillows we had slept on. His back muscles protruded in the dim light, moved when he turned, moved back when he laid flat. My stomach was churning; I felt like I was going to be sick. My muscles seized up every few minutes, then let go, then seized again. They shook intensely underneath my skin. I could not hold my fingers straight, my hands trembled so violently. I looked at my hands. It felt as though my body was crawling in beetles, like my skin was flaking off, separating itself from the muscle underneath. I held my stomach and rocked my naked form back and forth. My brain, a throbbing hunk of tissue, felt bludgeoned. My mind remembered the transcendence of the drug, while my body, torn and ragged, ached for death.

The smell of what we had done was the most poignant feature that marked the room. It was a faint smell, but it was undeniable. The smell of dried fluids, though organic in their composition, had transformed, changed by time into something completely different, something completely dead, cold, alien to the human body, and yet there.

The hall was dark and silent. I did not know what time it was. I presumed it had been hours since we had taken the Drips, but I could not ascertain the time. Where is Isabelle? I thought to myself. I heard a rustling from one of the alcoves. I stepped behind a piece of fabric and covered myself. I peered out into the darkness through a slit in the fabric. In the room there was a tall man, constructed of large muscles, and sharp bones. I looked beside him and saw Isabelle curled into a ball, sleeping in a heap of pillows.

His hands were large but nimble; they maneuvered the silver buttons of his shirt quickly. He put on a coat that fell to his knees and a top hat that covered his head. He wore a silver pin that reflected the amber light of the gas-lamps hanging above him. He stretched himself to the sky and let each of his muscles breath. My blood coursed through me rapidly, seething with rage. I watched him, knowing he could not see me. He looked my way. I did not recoil; the darkness hid me well. His face was decorated with beautiful full lips. The man left the room.

I walked over to the alcove where he had been. Isabelle was asleep.

Large almond eyes, bright red lips, she slept naked, curled in a ball. I picked up one of the pillows next to her and smelled it. The man smelled of tree bark and musk, not disgusting, but aged, mature, like a good bottle of scotch, or the scent of a cheese that at first seems repulsive but with time can become indulgent, even decadent, to the trained nose. I breathed him in, his aroma filled me, I memorized the scent so as to recall it another day. I looked down at the space and noticed a small white card on the ground. It must have fallen out of his wallet. I picked it up. I flipped the white card over, a business card. Dr. Remington, Psychiatry. How fortunate, I thought to myself as I smiled with satisfaction. I would find him again, I was sure of it. I wanted to gut him with a knife, as he had done to Isabelle with his penetrating sex. Isabelle stirred.

XI

Were you watching me? Isabelle questioned as she wrapped herself in a silk robe.

No, I… yes, Isabelle.

Do you think less of me, Blum?

We sat on the floor where they had coupled, where two bodies had entwined into one. I was sitting in the place where he had taken her, had enjoyed her for the first time, like I had long ago.

Isabelle, I started and then fell silent as I brushed her hair away from her face. There is little you could do that would make me think less of you. There are things we have sacrificed and things that we will sacrifice for our cause. Answer me though, what did you feel when you slept with him?

She wrapped a shawl around herself and tucked her knees into her chest. I lit two cigarettes and passed one to her.

She spoke: Nothing, Blum. You must understand that I did not do this for myself. There was no pleasure in this betrayal of my body. She held herself in a tight ball. This is rather a means to an end. It was the same with St. Ignatius. My ears perked up.

How so? I asked inquisitively.

I do not love St. Ignatius, Blum. There are many things that a woman can do to make a man fall in love with her façade, her image, her appearance, her motions, her caresses, the illusion that she knows the man desires to see.

A waft of smoke blew away from her plump lips. I wondered if this was an illusion she was presenting for me, or if this was in fact Isabelle. Was I too just a means to an end?

She continued: St. Ignatius led us here and it is here that we will find the source of the Offering. I cannot do this without you. You must be strong for me.

You know I am here for you, Isabelle. Only for you. I replied.

And the cause? She was hidden by a cloud of orange smoke.

Your cause is mine. I am your attendant. She smiled at me. It faded quickly.

Blum it is here that we will understand how the Magistrates have poisoned the world above. It is here that we will be able to subvert them.

And the man you were with, who was he? How does he figure into the cause? I asked her.

I could ask the same of you, Blum. I bowed my head low, regretted my actions of the prior night. Do not go sampling Jex's wares without knowledge of his intentions. I am sure Jex sees you as something else now. It is dangerous to open yourself to a man so quickly.

I know, Isabelle. That was not like me. It was the Drips. I had no knowledge of what I was doing.

I know, Blum. Do not be so quick to act when your emotions are tested. She lifted my head in her hand. I saw the way you looked at me. I know it was displeasing to see me talk to Jex like that. She let go of me.

It was, Isabelle. It was. I whispered.

You must know though that we are in grave danger, the man I laid with is a very powerful man. If he knew of my intentions, our intentions, he would have us killed.

What are our intentions, Isabelle? I asked cautiously.

Revolution. She mouthed the word at an inaudible level. Dr. Remington, like most men, is quite generous with information in his excitement. He has begun to tell me of the control he administers above. He has, even after just one night, confided in me.

What is it that he has told you, Isabelle? I asked impatiently, jealous of the secret they shared.

Though his intelligence, his projects, his experiments are genius; he is not wise. He is older than both of us, but he is not wise. Age does not determine wisdom. Wisdom blooms from the soul. She took my hand and placed it on her beating heart.

What experiments do you speak of? I interrupted.

He holds much sway over the Magistrates' scientific affairs. He has provided counsel for them before.

It is odd that a man of such prestige would frequent a place like this, I said.

Isabelle looked at me. It is not odd, Blum. It is human nature to want to explore what is forbidden, is it not? Even you Blum, though I know you had no choice, have learned anew the positions your body can take, the feeling of submission that another man can evoke in you.

I would have felt ashamed yet I could tell that she was not judging me but rather remarking that we both had sold ourselves for the cause.

Do you now understand why we are here, Blum?

I nodded. I love you, Isabelle, I said quietly. I was not sure if she heard me for she did not respond at first. She stood up.

It is unwise to love, Blum, she replied. It is unwise to love someone that is fated to die so young. She began to walk away.

I grabbed her arm and pulled her back into the alcove. I smelled like Jex. I was certain she could smell him on me. I took her head in my palm like she had done with mine. I took her hair in my other hand and stroked it, divided the matted parts, wiped away the makeup smeared around her eyes. I wanted so badly for her to know how much I loved her.

I pulled her up without warning, pulled her up close to me. I parted her robe and cast it aside like a snake does old skin. She was naked as she held me. I leaned into her, leaned my full weight into her sex. I pulled, held, and repositioned her body to suit mine. I manipulated her legs, reconfigured her arms, her neck, her ankles. She screamed, gave herself fully to me. She cried, her tears rolled down my lips, my chest, my thighs. As we climaxed, we reached a zenith, a point of height I had never experienced before. When I closed my eyes, I remembered the small, frightened girl I had rescued years ago. Here she was once again, asking for my aid.

The way that time passed in Jex's den was quite different compared to the regimented schedule of the world above. The people of the night slept often, ate less, and enjoyed the bodies of others voraciously, as if they could not live without the touch of another, as if the skin they touched nourished them like the food they did not desire. I belonged to Jex and to Isabelle. I desired her with every moment that Jex used me. She on the other hand had become the sole concubine to Dr. Remington. As I watched them over the months enjoying of each other, I could tell the power she held over him.

The smell of the man called me from behind the curtains. As he passed by my secret alcove, I inhaled his musk. My heart began to beat quickly. Pangs of anger sent shivers through my body. My hands shook; I was barely able to grasp the drink I was holding. I swallowed large gulps of liquor. The burn did little to settle my nerves. I watched him through a part in the curtain. I hid like a snake in a hole. I watched him pick Isabelle up by the waist and kiss her rose lips.

He greeted Isabelle with a smile. He brought her a bouquet of lilies; they mixed with his odor to produce an intoxicating aroma. As Isabelle grabbed him and whispered in his ear, a rage began to boil underneath my skin.

I heard her whisper: Dr. Remington, these flowers are so beautiful. I don't deserve them. I didn't know there were any flowers left in the Capital?

He replied in a deep voice, ancient like the mountains, an echoing voice: For some there are still flowers.

The flowers disgusted me, as I am sure they disgusted Isabelle too. She held him tightly. She extended her tongue from her tight little mouth and licked his neck, sucked gently on his right earlobe.

My pulse quickened, I wished so badly to be that man, to be the object of her affection. I wanted to stab his head with an iron spike and lick the blood from his skull. I wanted to completely devour him so that Isabelle would desire me in the same manner she desired him.

Come with me, Dr. Remington. Would you like to indulge in a bowl of Orange-Labyrinth before we begin?

Certainly, he replied.

Isabelle led him down the hall, her small hand grasping his larger one. They settled into an alcove down the way.

My heart was racing. I had to be still and silent. I moved like a quiet wind. I peeked at them from the adjoining alcove. She massaged his naked chest and shoulders from behind as he took deep, thick inhalations of Orange-Labyrinth. She undressed herself fully, let down her brown hair. It hung down to her breasts, which rested on his shoulders. She wore a belly chain of crystals that matched her large sparkling earrings.

When they began, I could not look. I filled my glass up with liquor from the bar in the alcove. I watched the girl maneuver herself onto the doctor. It was torturous. I longed so badly to be him. My stomach continued to twist and I swallowed more and more of the dark liquor. My head began to reel, to spin. As I continued to drink, my thirst for Isabelle grew. My sex wanted nothing more than to relieve itself with hers.

They were finished. I was finished. I laid back in the pillows and dreamed of laying next to her once more. I dreamed that I might lay with her and touch her soft body, like Jex had touched mine. I missed her even as she laid nearby. I heard them getting dressed. I heard him saying goodbye. She thanked him for his visit. It was very business-like, very perfunctory, the way she kissed him farewell and smiled while he exited. She clutched the clip filled with bills, marked with the three black dots of the Democracy. The encounter felt nothing like romance. I was relieved that she did not appear to have feelings for him. My heart and breath calmed down. I watched him as he left, followed him from afar to the exit. I had not been outside in weeks.

I approached Isabelle. Jex came over to us.

You do know who that was? He asked, with a smirk on his face.

He is an exquisite patron, Isabelle said to Jex as she handed him the money clip.

He purchases the Dust for the Magistrates' Offerings, Jex whispered. It is how this place continues to exist. It is how I continue to prosper. I owe much to that man and to the Dust.

I was surprised at how casually he imparted the knowledge to us. I reevaluated Jex's desire for me. Jex inhaled a burst of Dust from a small green bottle. When turned upside-down the bottle measured out one dose of the Offering. I yearned for the bottle he held. Isabelle quickly grabbed my hand and then released it, reminded me of my oath.

Dr. Remington mentioned to me his high standing with the Magistrates, Isabelle said. He has invited me to accompany him to the Magistrates' Golden Council, to partake in the official Offering. He has taken a particular liking to my skills.

I am not surprised, Isabelle. I must warn you, he is a very dangerous man.

Jex put his arm around my shoulder and I felt sick to my stomach. He ran his hands across my abdomen; it sent chills up and down my body. It is best that Blum accompany you.

I have sent girls with the doctor before. They did not return. The doctor is quite fickle. He is interested in the human body for love one day, and for science the next. I would not be surprised if he has made monsters out of the whores that I sent with him. Jex chuckled to himself.

We will go together, I said to Jex. I looked at Isabelle and nodded.

Yes, we will go together, Blum, she said with a smile.

☺

Isabelle dressed me. I remember it with a kind of clarity that only pure concentration, the pure unfolding of memory can provide.

Blum, you are a brave man.

She was in control. I looked admiringly at her breasts that sat perfectly on her chest, two luxurious mounds of soft flesh. She dressed me in the tuxedo that Jex had lent me for the occasion. I was a black and white clown. I would sing and dance and perform for her.

She continued: It takes a different kind of man to realize when a revolution is called for. I fumbled with my bow tie while she put on her black dress. She worked at putting an onyx, diamond, and silver clip in her short black wig. The clip sparkled in the yellow light of the den.

I am no revolutionary, I said.

I looked into the mirror as we dressed. Beads of sweat formed on my brow. She fastened dangling silver earrings to her ears and set an old silver necklace on her throat. The necklace erotically caressed her throat like I had wanted to, like I had done to her a hundred times in my dreaming fantasies. I noticed a birthmark on the side of her neck that I had not seen before. Though some would have called it a blemish, it radiated a pure sense of imperfect perfection that only the truly beautiful exude.

I continued: I have taken a man's life before. I'm not afraid. I thought I might be afraid, but I'm not. Next to you I am strong.

I looked at her through the mirror's reflection. Her lips were red, smoothed over with slick gloss. They shimmered in the low lights and orange smoke.

In this moment, I finally understand my purpose. I wrapped myself in the black cloak and placed the golden mask over my face.

Yes, she said. You saved me once before, and you will again. You are my liberator. Bring the people what they don't even know they are being denied. You are a prophet.

My muscles stiffened and my heart raced. It was intoxicating the way she massaged me with her words.

Lead the people to their freedom; they will thank you for it.

With that she came up behind me, hugged my hips with her dainty hands, pulled her waist into my buttocks. It thrilled me, filled me to the brim with excitement. I feared that I might overflow with the vitality of the moment. It was then that she opened my palm and moved the gun from her hand into mine. In her green eyes, I was a revolutionary, a prophet, a liberator. I repeated her words in my mind.

She let go of the gun, looked at me in the mirror, and whispered into my ear: Here is your sword, my liege.

XII

The dark cloak hid me from the crowd gathered on the balcony. The golden mask blended perfectly with those of the bureaucrats and Lesser Magistrates that surrounded me. I looked down at Isabelle from the balustrade as she and Dr. Remington sat amongst the chosen people. Rows of pews crossed the octagonal room from one side to the other. The High Magistrate's throne sat empty. It sparkled in the multicolored light streaming through the stained-glass window behind it. Those being honored by the Magistrates were to accept the divine Offering from the High Magistrate himself. Their faces were the only ones that would be exposed to his holiness. As Isabelle's protector I watched the scene impatiently from above.

Only the elite were allowed to indulge in the High Magistrate's Offering. Government officials, military officers, bureaucrats, administrators, civil and public servants, the Higher and Lower Magistrates; all were present. They were porcelain dolls, perfectly made up. Their hair curled about their faces. Their eyes sparkled in the cascading light of the chandeliers. The porcelain dolls chatted on, bobbed their heads, and drank endless goblets of wine. I debated the perfect moment to strike.

The gun felt foreign to my hand. It was heavy inside my coat pocket. I was sweating. It was hot under my cloak and mask. Isabelle flirtatiously toyed with Dr. Remington. She touched his leg. I will do anything for her, I thought. I perspired and trembled. The agitating moments passed by more like years rather than seconds. I heard the clock ticking. I stared at her red fingernails, manicured, delicate, tapping his knee as she waited in anticipation. The time of judgment would soon be upon us.

I heard the clock strike twelve as the High Magistrate took the podium to address the crowd of dignitaries. My hands shook as I groped for the gun in my jacket. I knew that she was waiting for me to pull the metal trigger. Outwardly she smiled, though I knew inside she understood the severity of the moment, the anarchy our actions would bring.

He was an average-sized man, with a deep booming voice. He was at least sixty years of age. He was hidden by his red judicial robes, which were marked by three black dots forming a triangle. He wore a monocle rimmed in gold that sparkled in the light of the crystal chandeliers. The clock was ticking.

He spoke: Our nation, the Unified Democratic League of Provinces, guided under the brilliant leadership of the Magistrates and their ubiquitous and loyal servants, personnel, clerks, and combatants was founded for the sole purpose of providing the people a nation where civility, justice, and strength are the pillars of daily life. The audience cut him off with cheers and applause.

He continued: We have purged the world of the poisonous people, the heathens, the maleficent, the vermin that crawled the city streets for too long. The clapping began again, washing out his next phrase. We have created the greatest nation in the history of humankind. A round of applause and cheers filled the room, mixed with laughter and sighs from ladies. It is with much honor that I present the graciousness of God upon those that have gathered here tonight. It is only through God's divine presence that we have collected here to celebrate. Join me. He shouted the mantra: Civility. Justice. Strength.

I gripped the gun, my eyes burned furiously as the words flowed out of his mouth and the mouths of his followers.

Civility. Justice. Strength.

I could tell Isabelle was wet with desire, wet for the red doom, the spray of blood and chaos that would soon fill the room, instead of the High Magistrate's propaganda and lies.

Civility. Justice. Strength.

I was sweating; my shirt was sopping wet. I wiped my brow with my sleeve. Isabelle quickly glanced up toward the balcony where I was stationed. Dr. Remington followed her glance and nodded his head towards the second story crowd. I could tell she was impatient, wanted to climax sooner than I was ready to. I was nervous, but not afraid. The High Magistrate continued, hushed the crowd with his wrinkled and twisted hands. I watched his hands closely, the same hands that signed bloody orders and decrees.

He spoke: Gentlemen and ladies of the party, silence. There is more work to be done. There is more justice to spread across the globe. You must understand that there is a grand solution at play here. The faces leaned in with interest. Though we have subdued the Red People, there is a world of heathens that remains to be saved. Domination and control, these are the keys to maintaining our power.

It is with great pleasure that I announce the unveiling of a project that has been in research for many years now. Thanks to the great contributions of Dr. Remington. Many faces turned around and looked at the doctor and his concubine, my Isabelle.

The High Magistrate continued: We have entered a new phase of our grand solution. A day of true purity is around the corner. There will be no disease, no imperfection, nothing but a race of Overmen to lead our great nation towards a world of salvation, a paradise upon this earth that only purity may bring.

I did not fully understand what he meant. My brain boiled inside of my skull. Cheers and praise. It was time.

I unleashed the gun from my pocket.

Suddenly, the stained glass windows behind the High Magistrate shattered into a kaleidoscope of different colors. I hid the gun next to my side as the room exploded into a panic. Without any warning, white-hooded figures leapt into the room on long braided ropes. A swarm also crashed through the windows lining the nave of the building. St. Ignatius' revolutionaries had arrived.

The Black Boots guarding the ceremony raised their guns and began to fire at the intruders. Some of the bureaucrats filling the pews cowered while other dashed out of their seats trying to escape. One man was accidentally shot straight through the temple, his lifeless body spilled over the pew he had risen from.

The trespassers left no time for deliberation. With loud howls they drew swords and pistols from under their robes. They began to massacre the crowd below. The upper balcony undulated with seething energy and I felt as if I was going to be thrown from the upper deck.

From below, Isabelle convulsed in a passionate culmination of emotion. I pulled the gun out again, aimed, and shot. This is the end,

I thought, the end of the corruption. I was caught inside a blur of sounds and motions.

Isabelle yelled: Shoot him, shoot him.

The bullets streamed across the great room, blasted past porcelain face after porcelain face. I struck a blow, the High Magistrates' left arm flailed backwards, as he toppled to the ground. I did not see where my succeeding shots landed. I fired bullet after blind bullet towards the stage, towards the crowd, hit others along the way but did not care. A primal rage guided me towards my imminent death.

In the mania, Isabelle pulled a blade from her thigh and stabbed Dr. Remington square in the chest. His body seized as blood poured out of his wound. In an unexpected burst of movement, Dr. Remington thrashed about and slammed his fist into her delicate skull. Isabelle slid to the floor in a crumpled heap.

The marionettes ran by me screaming, unaware of the source of the gunfire. The white-hooded figures leapt about the room swinging their blades wildly into the aristocracy that filled the lower level. The Black Boots continued to fire at them, smoke wafting up from their guns. The High Magistrate crawled on the floor towards safety.

In the chaos my fingers tightly clutched the gun as I aimed to deliver the final blow. As I pressed down on the trigger someone pushed me from behind and sent me flying into the mass of frenzied people. I could not fight the stampede of golden masks I had become a part of.

Before I was swept away, I turned back to look one last time. Dr. Remington was nowhere to be seen. The Black Boots had subdued the revolutionaries. Many people were sprawled out bleeding to death on the stone floor. A flurry of mixed limbs and blood was scattered across the room.

I saw Isabelle. Her body was surrounded by a group of Black Boots. Her wig fell off her head as they bound her. Isabelle's wounded cheek bled over her nose and lips. The High Magistrate had retreated into the darkness.

Blum, Blum, Isabelle screamed.

She was helpless as the Black Boots carried her body away, as well as the few surviving revolutionaries. They held her high over the throng of sneering and angry faces, bound, unable to move. Before I escaped amongst the chaos of the crowd, became one with the darkness, I saw the white hood torn from one of the captured prisoners. St. Ignatius lowered his head, blood spilling from a wound in his side.

⊙

While holding onto Zarian's dead body, I looked at the city before me in the distance. The man's soul was no longer with me. I thought of Isabelle and of the Midnight Man. I hoped that he would employ whatever necromancy was needed to restore her spirit. I desired one final caress of her nymph-like form before my eternity of servitude. I stood up and looked about myself. Yes, I had arrived. The Capital, that great metropolis, lay only a few miles ahead.

Part II

Metropolis

I

In the darkness I heard him breathing. I knew who it was, the cold draft, the aroma of brandy, the faint movement of shadow upon shade. Black tendrils of smoke curled about his form as he brought himself closer to me. There was no moonlight to illuminate his hidden face. He did not make a sound. I peered out at his figure, melting and congealing, pooling around my frail body seated inside the ash.

Have you come to take me? I questioned the darkness.

Like leaves falling from black crooked trees, his words scraped against each other as they fell towards me.

Blum, there is still more time for you, my son, my student, my angel of death. There are still grains of sand inside your hourglass. There is time yet for you to redeem the girl.

I did not like the way he spoke to me. I am no angel of death, I whispered.

You must be more observant, Blum. You must understand the role you play in this cosmic theater, he laughed. His laughter bellowed across the land. The wind blew small grains of sand into my eyes. I rubbed them clear.

I spoke: Why have you come to me?

You must understand the nature of your fate if you are to serve me upon your death.

Speak, demon, or leave me to my task, I said.

There are many who live their lives seeking a means to an end.

I recalled Isabelle referring to St. Ignatius, Jex, and even Dr. Remington as her means to an end.

For most, life is a series of obstacles that one overcomes or is stopped by. It is a series of minutiae strung together haphazardly to form opaque meanings, loose connections, and supposed loves.

When most people die they are tossed back into the current to be born again. There are others yet, who are lost, their souls remain bound to earth. They must be redeemed. Their tasks must be finished; their souls must be put to rest before they may enter the stream once more. Such is the case with your Isabelle.

There is a rare phenomenon that occurs no more than once every few hundred years. It determines how I must pick my servant; it is how I must choose who will take over my throne beneath. I stared at him, but could not discern any features. His darkness covered the landscape, impeded my sight.

My soul cannot rest until my successor is found. I see much of myself in you, Blum. I feel the passion and rage issuing from inside your beating heart. The strand of your life vibrates between my forefinger and my thumb. I have felt the pulse that courses through you. You are to take my place.

I do not understand. I am destined to be a devil such as you are?

He continued: Yours is a life of tragedy, Blum. Yours is a life not too dissimilar to the one I lived many ages ago. You have tasted death since the moment of your birth. You sent your mother bleeding, ripped in two, back into the stream when you were born. Even now you take the lives that wedge themselves between you and your love, or should I say, lust for Isabelle.

That is not true, I love her. I do love her. I love her even now as I sit here in the ash. I love her with every step I take. I love, my voice was hidden under the shaking gales of wind.

Your potential for death grows stronger each and every day. It fortifies the curse that thrives within you. It is the very reason why I have chosen you out of the millions of others to nurture, to cultivate for my role. Everything you touch has died. Everyone you will touch will die. Look at the dead man beside you. Your curse has broken him. Is it not because of you that your beloved died at the hands of the Magistrates? You failed to rescue her from death.

There was no way to save her. I could not reach her. It would have been impossible. My voice rose in defiance, as did the wind.

There are others that will die too, Blum. Is that not what you seek on this journey, more blood, more death? Yours is a life cursed by death. It is this that has brought me to you.

Cursed by death? I did not understand the demon's words.

Yes, Blum. I have seen your fate. You are doomed to end your days in misery, as I once did. You cannot change your fate. You have already signed away your soul to open your fate to the heinous acts that are before you. You have tasted death and you will taste death once more.

What heinous acts, you foul creature? I screamed.

He whispered his next words: A foul creature is what you will become, Blum.

You lie.

I was afraid that my accusations might cause the spirit to become angry, but like stones passing through air my words did not touch the Midnight Man. He leaned in, and I felt the cold coming forth from his breath.

Why would I lie to you, Blum? Think of me as your mentor, your brother, your father.

I backed away from him.

You don't know what you speak of, demon; you are no father to me. I have no father.

You have much to learn, Blum, too much to learn about the nature of your reality.

He stepped forward out of the dark. He paused and lit a cigarette. The fire from his match did not reveal his hollow and darkened face, but I saw the manicured suit and white gloves that I had seen once before.

Why is it that you lie to me, torture me so?

I am looking at the one who will take my place, Blum, the one who will relieve the burden and the curse that I have felt for too long. It is in you that I see the same destiny. It is in you that I see the completion of my fate and the beginning of your own. Your desire for revenge will affirm the curse that hangs heavy upon you.

There was an eerie silence and I thought I could make out the shape of two sunken eyes hidden inside the hood of blackness that covered his head.

Why me? I spoke, nearly defeated. Why did you not tell me of this sooner? You tricked me into this destiny.

He spoke: It was no trick. You entered into this contract willingly.

For the salvation of the girl if you recall? It is I that has kept you alive along this journey. You will have your revenge, Blum.

You are a demon. How could you resign me to this fate? I shouted violently at him.

Watch your words, Blum, for you have sealed your own fate. You have and will continue to succumb to your own curse. There is no changing the destiny you have made for yourself.

I will not end up a midnight shade, I cried out into the raging wind, but the Midnight Man was gone, vanished as quickly as he had come.

I awoke, covered in the loose ash, Zarian dead beside me, the city ahead. I reckoned it had been a dream, a nightmare, a hallucination brewed up by my desiccated brain. Yet, I could not shake the feeling of dread upon me, could not shake the memory of the darkness that whispered to me in the night. Still, memories of other ghosts were more pressing; and my Isabelle, whether I was cursed or not, would still be the benefactor of my retribution.

I will make the most of my time before he comes again, I said to myself as I marched on in the dark.

As I approached the city, it appeared different than how I had remembered. I climbed on top of the last of the ash dunes to look down into the Capital before me. It was a drab green, coated in dust and smoke. The great waterways were polluted; the streams and levies which once branched out from them appeared dried up. The channels were filled with urine and waste.

I drew closer and walked the streets lined in old gas-lamps. The Capital's denizens sunk into alleys and ditches, looked at me from the

darkest shadows of ill-lit corners. They crouched alongside brick buildings covered in a patina of mold and soot. As I followed the dark walls
of the Third Quadrant, I heard the rush of trains buried far beneath the
city. Accompanying them were the cries of men, women, and children
fading up through the steam vents sprouting out of the asphalt streets.
Everywhere, as I turned corner and boulevard, flags blew relentlessly
in the ash-littered air, great red flags with three black dots forming a
triangle.

It had been years, but I planned to return to Jex's den. I had nowhere
else to go. I wondered if Jex still considered me a friend. It would be
unwise for him to harbor a criminal, especially one as notorious as
myself, but I had no choice. I took some discarded rags from a nearby
trash bin and wrapped myself in them. I hid my face in a makeshift
hood that I had crafted from a piece of stained burlap. As the burlap
brushed the edge of my ear, I recalled the way she had once pressed
burlap so closely to her own skin. I remembered the dress had been too
small, remembered the innocence with which she wore it. I smelled the
material hoping it might contain some essence of Isabelle. It reeked of
foul garbage.

I hobbled down the alleys in the disguise. I picked up an old piece
of plastic piping and used it as a cane, painting the illusion of a much
older man. My weathered skin, parched from the desert trek, appeared
ancient in the dim glow of the passing gas-lamps.

I wondered how Jex had faired after the revolution had failed. I
wondered what had become of him once Dr. Remington recalled that
we were amongst Jex's most trusted concubines. Yet, Jex was not to
blame. He did not know the plans that Isabelle and I had created under

the guidance of St. Ignatius. He did not realize the extent to which Isabelle and I were going to stir the pot of anarchy.

Jex had loved me once. I prayed that he would still love me, or at least take pity on my soul. I hoped that Jex could help me locate Dr. Remington, so that I could take my revenge on the first of Isabelle's torturers.

I covered my face as I walked past a group of Black Boots. Red hats, a steady march of red hats, all doubles of each other, held the city together like muscle holds skin to bone. I stopped at the corner of the street underneath an overhang and leaned on the wall of a building. I picked through a garbage pail and ate the scraps of old deteriorating meals. I dug through the trash, moving newspapers aside in my search. My eyes caught the headlines as I rummaged: *Invasion Attempts Thwarted! Magistrates Help the Homeless. New Developments in Prosecution of Terrorists.* A moldy piece of bread. A half drunken bottle of water. It had been ages since my body had accepted so many nutrients in one sitting. I tried to pace myself with the water, knowing too well the sickness that would follow if I gorged myself. I wet my lips and saved the rest.

I looked at the Black Boots as they passed. Isabelle saw their coming; she read the fate of the world like a book. Isabelle saw what most dared not to see. Though the revolution had failed, her legacy continued to live in me. I would enact our revenge.

Dawn was approaching and the streets were becoming crowded. I pushed past the faceless people. Out of the corner of my eye I saw a young girl. She wore an old coat; it was stained in places with dirt and oil. I slowed my pace as I approached the girl. She stood at the entrance to a very small and dark alley, observed the passing traffic with a pitiful eye. Her face was dirty and stained with mud. The small girl contrasted greatly with the black suits whirling by her. She made eye contact with me. Her eyes were deep green.

I stopped and watched her from the shadows of the street. She was homeless. Her father had likely served in the war and died. I imagined her mother's body rotting inside the mass graves a few miles north of the Capital. Her clothes would have been endearing if they had been new, if they had not been doused in the sick smell of sweat and urine.

It was then that the Black Boots came out of the shadows from the alley behind her. My heart jumped. I moved closer. One of them cupped his hand over her mouth and lifted her up. Her legs kicked and body jerked wildly. She could not scream. She bit down on his hand but he did not let go. People passed by ignoring the struggle. I started to sweat. I stepped closer.

The other Black Boots followed her as she was carried deeper into the alley. I stood at the mouth of the passage, watching as they circled her.

The Black Boots laughed at her and shouted: Little bum, where's your mum? I'd like to show her a thing or two. They laughed and laughed, keeled over with laughter. Why are you crying, little girl, don't you have anybody to play with? I'll give you something to play with. They guffawed.

I closed in on them. The Black Boots were partially shadowed, but even so, they were repulsive. Their faces were pocked with sores, most likely caused by a venereal disease, which had become a growing concern. One grabbed her by her hair; another covered her mouth and pulled her to the floor. The girl was so young. Streams of blank faces continued to pass by the opening to the alley. The girl needed me.

I heard the Midnight Man whisper in my ear: Yours is a life cursed by death.

Excuse me sirs, I shouted as I interrupted them.

My heart beat ferociously in my chest. Two of the soldiers pinned the little girl down, and the third one was readying himself to penetrate her. Her clothes were pulled up. She looked helpless. A sense of overwhelming rage and dread filled me.

Piss off, the main perpetrator shrieked at me.

There are decisions you make in your life that can change the course of it completely. It was in that moment, when I saw the gnarled faces of her captors and witnessed her struggling to be free, that I changed forever. Silence overtook me. Blood filled my muscles. I felt a tingling sensation up and down my spine. I had reached an alertness that I had not experienced in years. It had been just one second, but it had been an important one. One I knew would change my fate forever.

It happened fast, a quick movement, a shove, and somehow I was in control. I felt the pistol, it was heavy, it was black. I pointed it, like I had so many years ago, and fired bullets into the man's chest. I blasted the fingers off another Black Boot's hand. He recoiled to the ground as a pool of blood quickly pulsed out of his body with each heartbeat. I showered another with bullets. His genitals blew apart and released a spray of red liquid into the darkness. His forehead, which had been grazed, had a large flap of skin hanging from it, and another bullet had pierced his right eye. With my remaining shots I splintered hip, thigh, and knee. It was fast, lasted only a few seconds. They did not scream for help, the shock and fear had paralyzed their tongues. Their blood cried out to me from the ground.

Blood pooled around the little girl. She did not scream. Rather, she balled her body up, hid from the tragedy that surrounded her. I was fascinated by the small child, the quiet child, the gentle child. She was not hurt. When the gunshots cleared she looked up at me, green eyes like seaweed, her body covered in gore. I would take the girl with me, and she would become a fugitive just as I was. Then she turned and ran down the shadowed alley. Isabelle's eyes had peered out of that small broken child. By some compulsion of fate, I chased after her.

She ran deep into the belly of the city. She crossed bridges, discovered the small places of the Third Quadrant. She jumped low walls and climbed staircases that wound up the sides of buildings. She climbed underneath dumpsters, between gates, and through holes I did not even know existed. She wanted so badly to get away from me. Then she stopped. She was pressed up against a brick wall, hemmed in on all sides by tall buildings. The shadows of those buildings loomed over us and created a deep darkness in the morning sun. The buildings were roofed with copper panels. The gutters were made of copper too, turned green from exposure to the elements. The gutters wound their way into the alley. A trickle of water ran down the wall the girl hunkered beside.

I don't want to hurt you, I said. I am trying to protect you.

I paused. She did not respond.

Where are your parents?

The girl did not move. I reached my hand out to touch her shoulder. She shivered at my touch. She turned her face to meet mine. Her eyes, luminous even through the darkness, caught mine. I have seen those eyes before, I thought. They were deep, vibrant green, noble eyes. Isabelle's eyes stared back at me.

It's going to be okay, I said, trying to make her less afraid of me.

I pulled her coat over her shoulders. She brought her hands out from within her huddled form. In her hands she clutched a small white rabbit. Its neck had been snapped in two. I looked into its dead, glazed over eyes. I wondered how its fur remained white, when she had been covered in filth. I wondered if it had been her pet.

I won't hurt you, I said.

She remained silent. I nodded my head to show that I understood her silence. A compassionate smile spread across my face.

I made her leave the rabbit in the alley. I think she understood that it could no longer help her; she would no longer have to rely on it for company, friendship, and camaraderie.

In times of strain the living cling to memories of the dead. It is the curse of the living to remember the dead, to awaken each day and obsess over the disagreements they could not settle with the dead. I wiped a delicate piece of ash away from her forehead.

I will call you Asha, I said. I took her hand in mine and led her away from her past.

II

As we passed a group of Black Boots, Asha and I hid inside the broken colonnades that lined the city streets. They did not notice us. They looked across the street into a small window. A young woman was changing her dress in plain view. They gawked at her curves silhouetted on the frosted windowpane. I did not let Asha know that I too desired the lady behind the glass.

I looked down at the child and recalled a time far gone.

The girl silently held my hand as I led us towards Jex's den. She understood that she would be my child. We walked in the cold tarp-covered alleys, dim-shadowed alleys, alleys where dripping water fell on our heads, alleys that smelled of rats and trash. We headed towards the slums.

Jex will keep us safe. The girl will just have to come along. She will adapt, I thought as I tightened my grasp around her small hand.

Stay close to me, I told her as we entered a hidden sewer drain that fed directly into Jex's complex. The sound of dripping water filled the hollow tube. Do not let go of my hand. Do not look anyone in the eye.

I could tell she was afraid, but she listened. She hung her head down low and readied herself. A small string of lights led us to a metal service grate at the end of a long sewer system. I knocked on the metal, the sound reverberated through the silence. I looked around to make sure that no one was following us. I knew Jex had cameras everywhere, I knew he had already seen us coming. I was hoping that the Black Boots didn't also have cameras in the sewers. The grating opened and we stepped through. We turned the corner and walked through a small wooden door. A cloud of smoke poured out into the tunnel. It smelled pungent, it smelled like Orange-Labyrinth, my mouth began to salivate. I looked at Asha; guilt soured my stomach.

A voice penetrated the mist: I thought you were dead, Blum.

When the smoke cleared I saw that it was Jex. A small man accompanied him. He wore a black coat that came down to his knees. Jex motioned for the man-child to move along and prepare some drinks for us. Jex's servant was deformed; he stooped over himself, his hand was pulled in close to his side, his knee buckled in an odd way that forced his whole left flank down toward the ground. He looked as if there was a weight pulling his small body down to the earth.

Come in, stranger. He smiled as he welcomed us in with a motioning hand gesture. Who is the girl? Is she for sale? He inquired.

No, I stopped him. I gave him a stern look. She is mine; her name is Asha. She will be coming in with me. No one is to touch her. Do you understand?

Of course, my friend. I understand. I won't touch her, Blum. I can't speak for the others; it's been a while since we've had any fresh meat down here. Asha looked up at me, I patted her head to let her know I wouldn't let anything happen to her.

Jex pulled back the last of the curtains partitioning the room and sat down at the head of a low circular bronze table. Four nude women took seats beside him. One of the women caressed his chest, while another stroked his right arm. His hands began exploring their exposed parts; when he remembered Asha was present he retracted them. Jex's servant placed drinks in front of us, and then moved and stood next to Jex so as to face Asha and me. Jex had aged, his teeth were badly stained from the Orange-Labyrinth that he delighted in. He smiled and motioned for me to sit while he lit a cigarette. I lit one, too.

I thought you were dead, Blum, or at least rotting away in some prison. You know you could have given me a little more warning that you and that bitch, Isabelle, were going to go shoot up the Magistrates. He looked me in the eyes. I don't like them either, Blum, but you have to understand when you're outmatched. How did you manage to stay alive?

That does not matter, Jex; I need a place to stay for a while. I know it's a lot to ask, but we have nowhere to go right now. I'll work for the rent. You know I'm good for it. Just a few days.

Secrecy seems to be your game, Blum. He paused and took a deep drag. I don't know. You're quite the liability. I don't want the Black Boots coming in here, messing up what I've got going. You nearly got me killed last time. If it wasn't for the Dust I would have been hanged. You understand don't you? He smiled, a large grin.

I did understand. I understood too well what Jex meant, he was not a person that cared for helping anyone unless he received something in return. The good thing about Jex was that he could always be bargained with.

Take whatever you want from me, Jex. Just don't touch the girl.

He looked me up and down. How you've aged, Blum. He paused. We'll clean you both up. You can stay. Three nights, then you're out.

Jex, Asha, a few of the concubines, and I sat at a low table. We sat on pillows on the floor. The smoke from the water pipe filled the room. I inhaled from the cord connected to its large glass base. The glass was filled with water that gurgled with every inhalation. Bubbles danced in the clear water. The water was tinted with a rich orange pigment. The smoke traveled up the metal shaft and through the rubber hose into my mouth. The rush of the drug was immediate. Unlike the Drips, there were no hallucinogenic properties associated with the mixture, but rather the imbiber was filled with a soft smoke that relaxed the eyes, the skin, and provided the sensation of floating, as if on a buoy out at sea. Asha looked at me as I sucked in the smoke and passed the cord to a small Oriental concubine that had taken a seat to the right of me. Jex pulled out a small chest from under the table and opened it.

What are you in the mood for today? I think the girl is a little too young to start sampling my wares, but I'm not going to tell you how to raise the little bitch.

I cringed at the word *bitch*, but did not show it. Asha looked down. Jex resumed stroking the woman next to him.

So, what'll it be: Dust. Drips. Try some of this Z-Pam. You'll love it.

No, I'm fine.

Suit yourself, Blum. Jex swallowed a blue pill. I thought you were dead, Blum. Am I talking to the walking dead? He looked me in the eyes, as his fingers nimbly pulled some more blue pills from under the table and deposited them in his mouth.

Consider me of the dead, I responded recalling my dark pact and the contract that I had signed. I wondered of the Midnight Man's honesty, of his true intentions, of the power he actually held over my mortal soul. He had hid the details of our agreement until he knew that I would not refuse. He had hidden the truth that I was to take his place until I had reached the Capital, until Zarian lay dead in the alkaline dust, until I was left alone. I wondered if there was more truth to be uncovered.

I could not surmise if he had intended for me to meet the child. She had, in just a short while, alleviated me of some of my desolation and grief. I took great joy in looking at her, the image of Isabelle cast in her small bones. If I was truly cursed, would the child not die as well?

Jex spoke: What will you do now, Blum? What are your intentions?

I thought a moment, picked up the small bottle of blue pills that Jex passed around the table. I read the label: Z-Pam; Uses: Induces conscious sedation, for extreme apprehension and panic disorder. I pocketed a few Z-Pam and passed it along. Asha did not notice. I looked at Jex as he fondled the woman beside him. She arched herself towards him, desiring his masculine fingers upon her breast, his forearm to caress her inner thigh.

I intend to finish what I have started, Jex, I boldly told him. He raised his eyes and his smile faded.

Blum, you are certainly a fool. There are men who have come up against the Magistrates before and they are now ash. You brought hell into my house once before, and if it were not for the doctor's fondness for my supply of Dust, I would be ash as well. He packed another bowl of Orange-Labyrinth, the cloud of smoke hid his face momentarily.

Your St. Ignatius, have you not heard of his fate? Jex's words sounded long. His stretched vowels matched the stretched curls of orange smoke that poured from his mouth.

I cannot say I have, I replied.

He looked to his side as he brought another concubine into his grasp.

Your precious Saint, my brother in vice, is but ash and dust, Blum. He is buried out in the desert somewhere. The Black Boots sent him away shortly after the inquisition. I've been lucky, Blum. If they were to discover that I have taken you in once again, that you have survived, they surely would not pardon me again. I take a great risk for you, my friend. You will not do your dark bidding while you are here with me. He paused. Have you come unnoticed?

Yes, the word caught in my throat as I remembered the Black Boots who murdered Zarian. Why Zarian had uttered my name in his final moments was a mystery to me. It would be but a matter of time before the Magistrates realized the desert had not consumed me, that I had taken up residence once more inside the city of rotted copper and stone, the great metropolis, the Capital.

You will come to my room tomorrow, Blum. For now you should clean yourself and take the child. Get some rest. There is food and water for you inside your quarters.

We entered our personal quarters. The small girl reminded me so much of Isabelle. Her hair, her eyes, her skin. I led her to the bathroom where she washed her hands, face, and body. I handed her the clothes Jex had left for us. They were too big for her. We ate the food and drank our fill of water. After, I washed myself, felt the water grace my bones. The girl slept in my bed. I watched her sleep. I watched her dream. I swallowed a Z-Pam and poured myself a large glass of dark liquor. I smoked a cigarette and watched her, wondering if in dream she was somehow communicating with the dead.

After my drink, I crawled into bed next to Asha and closed my eyes. It was hard to fall asleep. I felt the presence of the dead all around me, but when I opened my eyes Isabelle was nowhere to be found. I closed my eyes once more and she came to me.

⊙

I rushed away through the crowd of bureaucrats. Tears dropped profusely from behind the mask that hid my face, the face of an enemy, a traitor. I could not save Isabelle. I did not know where to turn, for the place that I had called my home, Jex's den, would certainly not be welcome to me after such an act of treason. I took residence in a dark alley, beside a dumpster. I smeared my face in the mud of the alley and waited. I heard the sound of Black Boots marching furiously through the streets, the sound of alarms issuing from poles and towers. The Capital was on alert and the frightened people walking the streets were met with brutal interrogation. The vigilant eyes of the High Magistrate were fixed upon finding me, a piece of refuse lying amongst an even larger pile of trash.

In the morning, there had not been too much change. The feeling of chaos remained throughout the city, and I only moved from the alley for fear that they might sweep the district where I hid. I climbed some rotting stairs to reach the top of a dilapidated building. I hid behind a makeshift wall overlooking a public plaza. I wanted to get a look at the anarchy I had wrought upon the Democracy, to comfort myself that Isabelle's capture had not been entirely in vain. Large screens had been set up to play a public service announcement to inform the people of the events of the prior evening.

The screens flickered on. The High Magistrate walked around a group of men wearing gold masks. He waved a censer back and forth, granted them a divine blessing. He hid his wounded hand inside his robes. His red garment flowed to the ground. I admired his technique, repeating the arcing action over and over in such a precise fashion, even though his other hand had been destroyed. I observed the calm fashion in which the High Magistrate commanded the group.

The Magistrate addressed the people in the plaza through the screens: Yesterday the Red People infiltrated my holy Offering service. I heard a gasp from the plaza. You need not worry, citizens. We have captured the woman responsible for the attack.

I felt my blood begin to warm. I desired to be inside the circle and to inhale the smoke from the censer as I cut him from top to bottom.

She will be dealt with, she is a traitor to the Capital and the Democracy, and she will be disposed of. Let this be a lesson to all, the Democracy will not tolerate dissent. The crowd cheered and received their daily Offering in acceptance of the words he spoke.

Citizens, do not be deceived. The heathens, the barbarians, they will try to deceive you. They will use their witchcraft to dissuade you from the teachings, the prophecies, the communications I have received from God and passed on to you.

As the High Magistrate spoke the word *God*, the men in the circle knelt down and started speaking the mantra. Their words did nothing to drown out the High Magistrate's loud voice.

The Red People will never defeat us. They will be eliminated, extracted from the breed of men. They will no longer poison us with their unclean seed. The speech became louder. Even Red People as beautiful as she will never succeed.

The robed men banged their hands on the marble floor, creating a slapping percussion that added to the tension in the plaza. Let us observe the demon we have captured.

The screen flickered and showed the inside of a white room. Dr. Remington stood beside Isabelle's body, which had been bound to a metal gurney. Though she struggled to escape, she could barely move. A red gag ball had been placed in her mouth.

Dr. Remington spoke: We assure you, citizens, we will find the others. We will make sure their leader and their kind are punished. As we wait for the others to come forward, this wretched woman shall suffice. It will not be a quick death. I have prepared some experiments for our fine specimen. It is but a matter of time before she will die. Nothing can save her. He paused and looked up from the girl, except perhaps if a different traitor should like to take her place.

I wondered how the doctor had survived. Isabelle's knife must have narrowly missed his heart.

We have dealt with the Red People, Blum. Dr. Remington had said my name. The people in the plaza looked puzzled, though they remained silent and listened to every word he uttered. We will deal with you as well. Do you love the girl? He started laughing as he touched Isabelle's neck and then her naked breast. She shook violently but she could not stop him from touching her.

Did you know that Isabelle is pregnant, Blum? Is the bastard yours?

Pregnant? My mind flooded with a surge of energy.

Come out, come out, wherever you are. He cackled, and slid his white gloves longingly over her throat. I imagined he took great pleasure in knowing that he would explore the woman like no man had ever done before.

Could the child be mine? I thought.

Blum, this is how we deal with traitors. You have time to come forward; we will not take her until her belly has reached a fuller form. He laughed again. Observe, this is how we have dealt with the rest of the Red People.

The screen cut away to an aerial view of a large gray complex. A fence surrounded it, made of steel poles, wrapped in gnarled, twisted rings of barbed wire. The bodies of the dead were strung up on lines, as if in their last moments they had thrown themselves up against the fence. They appeared like wet rags hung out to dry, left out in the elements too long, small balls of cotton caught on thorns, turned a putrid black. I imagined the smell of burnt hair and smoldering bone. I looked into the darkness behind the bodies and saw that great pits had been dug beside the barracks. Bodies were becoming other bodies, melting and molding into one another. The streets were not lined in lampposts, but rather the limbs of men. Their bones reached up towards the stars in one last desperate pose before death, like cornstalks rising from the earth before the reap.

Behind the fence stood the prisoners. With long ghostlike faces, they stood motionless, thin, starving. They were hunched over, held themselves in areas split and cracked by the dry wind. They suffered from malnutrition and carbuncles caused by pestilence. I imagined the stench of rotting meat. They wore rags, black and white rags, split rags that barely covered their bodies; bodies that were mostly bones, ribs, and joints. Bodies that were all skin, tightly mummified onto skeletons of long deceased corpses. The women had no breasts, the men no body hair. All of them were bald and their teeth were rotten. Their lips were colored white from the alkaline salts that blew through the compound.

This is what has become of the vile race of the Red People, the High Magistrate spoke over the revolting images. They are Jookies, the Red People, they are enemies, perpetrators, and thieves.

They did not look human, yet they were. I could not decide if they were beasts or men. They were fallen angels with cut and bleeding wings. I hoped Isabelle would not end her days like them.

The screen flashed back to the High Magistrate who had taken a seat on his golden throne. Citizens of the Democracy, never forget that they are our enemies. They are rats. They are not of the same flesh and blood as we are. Do not trust the voices of the liars. They have been locked away, hidden to protect the people, our citizens, our country, our Democracy. This is the solution to our problems with the west. This will bring the purification we desire, he bellowed. The land will be pure once again and our seed, the seed of our science and progress, will grow rampant like wildflowers in the field. Citizens, we rely on you to bring the other culprits forward. I felt his voice sinking into my brain. Citizens, remember that God has spoken to you today.

The film zoomed in on his gold-covered face, and he managed a discreet smile from his tight smoke-filled mouth before the screens went black.

☺

I awoke beside Asha. It was still night, still dark. I went to the bathroom to get some pills. I swallowed the Z-Pam. Despite the company of the small girl, I felt alone. The sharp edge of the razor dragged its way across my flesh, like the doctor's fingers had along Isabelle's throat. It stung, it bled. Drops of blood trickled down my forearm, down my elbow, jumped, bounced, and flew downward into the sink. Crimson rings formed and pushed outward to the edges of the sink. Muddied water, clumps of hair, the remnants of shaving cream all turned a light shade of red. I turned on the water and the drain swallowed all traces of my wound. I used some gauze to patch the damage.

I looked up into the bathroom mirror. I stared at my face. My skin was pale. Lines wormed across my once smooth white face. My eyes looked sunken from malnutrition. The mirror spoke to me: If you stand here long enough, will anyone come looking for you? The child perhaps. Will they notice if you break the glass and cut yourself? Asha would notice. I downed some pills and the mirror stopped talking to me.

I saw Asha appear in the mirror's reflection. How long has she been standing there? She was quiet, a pale ghost flickering behind me. Had she seen me cut myself? Had she seen me take the blue pills? As the pills dissolved in my stomach and entered my blood, the world began to fade away. My breath became shallow, my heartbeat soft, my mind blank, and I slept.

III

I remembered little of the incident in the morning. When we awoke it was nearly dusk. We had slept the day away. The days and nights were lost in Jex's den and since he had promised us only three nights, it was not long before we had outlasted his offer. As it happened, he did not ask us to leave, so once more I became a permanent fixture in his toxic world.

We were fed, Asha slept most of the time, and Jex and I reveled in his vast array of powders, liquids, and pills. The price I paid was small. I slept with Jex, when he desired me, and with Asha when he did not. I entertained him with tongue, belly, and eyelash, if that was what his craving called for, and in return Asha was left alone.

In the lonely hours of the day I taught Asha what I knew of self-defense. I showed her the weak spots of a man's body: groin, neck, and eye. I showed her maneuvers that could prove useful in the event that I was not there to protect her.

I did not speak to Jex's other concubines. They were mostly women who scowled at me when I passed by. They were jealous of the attention Jex paid to me; I knew that they observed his fondness for my body over theirs.

It was not a new experience for me to sell myself to survive. It was not the first time that Jex had eaten of me in that way. His bed, a giant floor full of goose down pillows and blankets, had welcomed me before. I felt him using me in a variety of ways, some new and others familiar. I knew he took pleasure in every hedonistic moment of our coupling, every moan, every scrape, every bludgeoning of limb into limb. Though I cried, he did not notice the tears in his state of ecstasy. He did not see my face behind the cloud of smoke that divided his musculature from mine. I felt his panting on my neck. Large breaths expelled from us, created invisible clouds of heat, like the rippling thermals that birds ride high into the sky. They passed before our almost touching faces, an invisible barrier that separated me from him and him from me.

My soul was not there in the stack of multicolored pillows. He grunted, screamed, and moaned. I felt myself playing the part. It was an art I had practiced and mastered. I heard myself flawlessly delivering the scenes of the play, heard myself panting, commanding, and submitting, but that was not where I desired to be.

My soul was afloat in the sky with Isabelle, high up where the birds glide and swoop about. There we saw cloud, sea, sun, and snow. Up in the mountains, high up where I knew I had never been before, where the birds cawed and sang mating songs, I felt free. As we rolled in the cloudbanks, draped ourselves in sunlight, smelled the crisp air of an elevation that only God himself could have created, I felt whole. In the underground of Jex's den, my body doubled over with gesture, position, and pain.

⊙

I stood up and left the room. The main hall was thick with stale smoke. I saw Asha sleeping on a bed of pillows inside one of the alcoves.

She was alone; she looked peaceful. Her hair was soft, it looked clean, it looked like fine strands of brown silk spun together, flaring out in all directions upon a pillow constructed of purple velvet. I let her sleep for the moment.

I went further down the hall clutching my naked form. Women slept inside the alcoves, some embraced the men they had enjoyed the prior evening, some were alone, some embraced each other, all of them were completely unclothed. I poured myself a glass of water. I was so thirsty. I swallowed the water in greedy mouthfuls, felt the liquid rush through my stomach and freshen my skin. I was grateful for the water.

I sat down next to the large low table and sank inside the stack of pillows. I filled the clay bowl with Orange-Labyrinth and lit the top with a smoking piece of coal. The inhalations deadened my mind to the baseness of my physical form. I felt the waves of air lapping up against my skin, pooling between my legs, inside my ears. The waves butted up against my sides, rippled alongside me like I was a great ship in the Magistrates' fleet.

I saw Jex standing in the doorway of his chamber. He came over to the table robed in brown velvet. He sat across from me, looked into my sorrowful eyes, and I could tell that he knew what I was yearning for. He knew I would never love him in the way that he so clearly loved me. He knew that I would always love Isabelle.

You are free to go, he mumbled. You know that, right? The girl and you can leave when you desire. I was silent as I sucked on the pipe and then passed it his way.

I know, I said in a low voice. I admire you, Jex.

Why is that, Blum? He looked shocked.

I admire the way you imbibe the human body. You can dance from one to another, from man to woman, like you have no care. It is hard to love, and it is hard to lose love.

You don't think I know that? He said sternly. You don't think I know what it feels like to yearn day in and out for something I know I can never have. He looked down. There is sadness in me, Blum. There is sadness like you wouldn't believe. Even though I have you now, I know it is Isabelle who occupies your mind. I know it is a matter of time before you will leave once more. I am powerless, Blum.

We were silent. The bubbles in the glass base of the water pipe gurgled.

I can't love you, Jex, I said after some time. I can't love anyone but her. I hope you understand. That is why you must help me. If you have love for me, like you say you do, you must let me go. Help me find the doctor. I must avenge her, Jex.

What about me, Blum? What happens to me when you leave? Where will the Black Boots look first? Where will they suspect you came from? I am taking a risk. I am taking a risk I know you will never repay. Yet, I am powerless not to take it. Tears fell from his closed eyes, fell from a face shadowed in orange light.

Jex, I spoke again when I began to feel the magical lethargy of the smoke settling in my brain.

Yes, he replied.

I looked over at Asha, she seemed so peaceful, so quiet, like a small animal that had been injured and needed the comfort of sweet dreams. I looked at her face. She seemed so much like Isabelle when she had been lying on the doctor's metal table, eyes closed underneath perfect almond lids. I looked back up at Jex.

You must know where the doctor is.

Yes, Blum. I know where your doctor is. I know, but in my knowing, in my telling, in my words I know that I hold the very key to my undoing. He looked up; his eyes were swollen and red. Yet, he paused, I will do it for you. If I bring the doctor here, you must promise me, Blum, that you will do nothing while he is in my den. You have to promise me that you will be able to control yourself. I will bring him here to enjoy one of the whores. He fancies an Oriental as of late. He will come. They will commit their act. Then you must leave, Blum. You are never to return. Follow him where you will. He held his head in his hand. You have certainly brought the devil to my door before. With this act, he will surely come again.

Jex stood up and left me alone at the table. I continued to smoke the Orange-Labyrinth, fixated on the sweet taste of the curling smoke, fixated on the rage I would unleash on the doctor. I imagined the feeling I might have when I could delve my knife into him, as he had done to Isabelle. Yes, I thought. The Midnight Man had been right. I am fated to a life filled with death.

I smiled and looked over at Asha. She had not stirred. She will come and hunt with me; perhaps the girl might have a role to play in my revenge.

⊙

The day was long, the night even longer. I sat smoking a cigarette in one of the entrance alcoves, which was hidden by colorful, draping curtains. I waited for Dr. Remington to arrive. Asha sat beside me. I liked the time we spent together. We did not communicate through voice, she had not uttered one word in all the days since our meeting, yet we understood each other quite well. I understood that when she was sad she liked me to hold her or stroke her hair. When she was shy, she would hide behind my legs and pretend to disappear, a wisp of air caught in a den of smoke.

I smelled him enter the room.

Asha, stay here, I whispered.

I put my finger to my mouth in anticipation and gently chewed at my nail. Asha stayed put, she dared not resist my request. She realized that she owed her life to me. She knew that even though I clothed, fed, and loved her, there was always the possibility that she could be sent back up to the streets. I had murdered for her. I had taken life and spilled blood for her. I had reinforced the Midnight Man's curse for Asha, all for her sea-green eyes, Isabelle's eyes.

The attraction between the concubine and the doctor was hormonal, raw, something to do with the pheromones floating through the air. He consumed her in the same way that he had consumed Isabelle. As I watched them couple, it did nothing to excite me. Quite the contrary, their primal act was bestial and I cared nothing more than to slaughter them like the bull and cow they were. As he prodded her, and she cooed for him, I began to chew at the inner lining of my cheeks. The sight of the two of them was disgusting, yet I could not look away. My eyes were fixed on her breasts and on the man's firm posture, as he gored the woman who was less than half his age. Their scent was even more disgusting. I chewed the flesh inside my mouth till I began to bleed.

It was over quickly. It seemed to be quite routine. Dr. Remington dressed. The used up whore laid splayed on the pillows beside him, eyes closed, avoiding awkward conversation. I saw the doctor glance in my direction. I recoiled as he continued to stare at the curtain where I was hiding. Can he see me? I thought.

My palms were sweaty. I grabbed an ice pick that was on a table behind me. I remembered the promise that I had made to Jex. I would not betray his trust; I would not kill the doctor in his den.

The movement of my digits seemed quite uncontrollable, yet I withheld my instinct to kill him. He drew closer to the curtain. He was so close, my hands were trembling as I gripped the pointed blade. I could have reached out and landed one clean blow to the arteries of his bulging neck. He stank. My mouth curled up at the corners into a foul grimace. I leaned into the curtain, my hands lifting above my head, the ice pick in hand. He drew even closer to the curtain as he fastened the final button of his coat.

Jex, Dr. Remington spoke firmly into the cavernous hall. I stood still and waited quietly. My knees trembled with the anticipation of his death.

Dr. Remington, so pleased you could come by this evening, I heard Jex's voice from behind.

I sank into the pillows of the alcove, threw the ice pick to the floor. I would wait.

Jex, I presume you know the state the Capital is in?

What state might that be, Dr. Remington?

Oh, so you have not heard? There are criminals on the loose above ground. A certain criminal from a time long ago is thought to have broken free from one of the chain gangs that were sent into the desert. The Black Boots are scouring the Quadrants for him. I trust you know nothing?

I could tell Jex was nervous.

I have heard nothing. What criminal? His voice was not as convincing as he had hoped it might be. Dr. Remington smiled at Jex and smoothed his hair. It seemed as though Jex knew far more than he was letting on. Dr. Remington's calm resolve and cool confidence almost brought Jex to a state of panic.

His name is Blum, you remember him, do you not?

I do, he replied. I have not seen him. I thought he was dead. Dr. Remington, you know I had nothing to do with the attack. Was the trial not enough? I told you everything I knew years ago. Jex backed up a couple steps, and the doctor followed him, pressing him into the wall.

I know, Jex. I know that if you were involved things would be different. After all, Jex, I am your friend. He had a devilish smirk on his face. I am your only friend up there. If it were not for me, and my program, you would have been gone long ago. Jex, you would not lie to your old friend would you? He closed in on Jex. Jex pushed himself up against the back wall.

Never, Jex stuttered.

I thought for a moment of intervening, of taking the ice pick and stabbing him from behind. However, I did not. I watched, hoping that the doctor would move away from Jex, who had taken Asha and me in against his better judgement.

Good, Dr. Remington backed away and started for the door. Jex breathed calmer the further the doctor got from him. Before he exited, Dr. Remington turned around one last time.

Oh, Jex, one more thing. It would be wise to keep a tighter leash on those that you employ.

As he slammed the front door I felt the urge to follow and strangle him in the alley. Jex turned white and after a moment silently returned to his quarters.

A few minutes after Dr. Remington had left, I motioned for Asha to follow me out of Jex's den. It was time. We had outstayed our welcome. We began to climb the steps to the ground level. Asha clung desperately to my hand.

Suddenly, a large blast sounded throughout the den, a hundred pipes backfiring in unison. Cymbals crashed, beams fell, the floor cracked in a thousand places. I looked back as I witnessed an explosion rip apart the bedroom Jex had returned to.

I threw Asha in front of me and pushed her up the remaining stairs, bits of debris flew all around us. The flames of the fire spread from drape to drape, turned the multitude of hanging colors into a thick black char. The pillows, rugs, and blankets blew apart with ease. I raced up the stairs listening to the screaming of the Oriental woman echoing throughout the den.

A brief look back: I saw her, head full of flame, a crown she would wear but once. Her skin flaked away, her eyes melted into two black balls, and her teeth, her lips having retracted, flashed a brilliant white smile in my direction before they fell limply onto the blazing floor.

I grabbed Asha and fled up into the streets in a panic. I did not see the doctor anywhere. As we escaped into the night, the den continued to explode underground, and smoke billowed high into the sky out of sewers and drains. The Black Boots were nearby. We clung to the alleys and the corridors; the shadows hid us well. I forced Asha to run, to remain quiet; I muffled her gasps for breath and her sobs as we searched for Dr. Remington. We combed the streets looking for Isabelle's murderer.

We raced through sewers, tunnels, and over bridges, two vagrants in the night, illuminated only by the moon and stars above. The firestorm raged behind us. It was then, as we stopped, panting in the darkness, I saw him, Dr. Remington, laughing to himself on his walk home. I knew then that the Midnight Man had answered my dark prayers. I grabbed the girl's hand and followed him down the dark alley. I felt the Black Boots on my heels. I held Asha with a tight grip. I did not want to imagine the consequences she would face if the Black Boots found her. We lurked silently in the shadows as we followed him. A number of blocks later he turned into a large stone building.

IV

Level fourteen. I watched him push the button and enter the lift. He smiled to himself in the neon lights of the hallway. Clutching Asha, I circled the structure to the side alley where a fire escape crawled up the side of the building. Most of the windows were dark. I jumped up and pulled the ladder down, it clanked and jangled in the silence of the night. I looked around myself, fearful that the Black Boots might have heard me. I forced Asha to scramble up the ladder, motioned for her to keep moving as I followed up behind her.

We reached the fourteenth level terrace. A grated platform spanned the side of each story of the building, allowing each room access to the fire escape.

We will sleep here tonight, Asha, I whispered.

I wrapped her in my coat. She will be fine, the child will be fine, I thought. I laid her down to go to sleep and I kissed her forehead. I looked at her eyes as they closed, her body shivered. I love her, I thought as I kissed her again.

Sleep well, I whispered as I stroked her hair.

When Asha was asleep I crawled over to the lit window and looked inside. The window was dirty. Gray soot was caked on it. The entire building, rather institutional in its construction, had become a victim of rot and neglect. Most buildings inside the Capital had lost their former beauty.

Inside the room there were two brown leather chairs, with a small wooden table between them. A bookcase lined the far side of the room. A doorway, presumably leading to the hall, was also on the wall. The door was painted red and its threshold was rounded into an arch. The doorknob was rusted brown; an engraving of a fleur-de-lis decorated its face.

On the right side, more bookcases and a large grandfather clock lined the wall. A golden pendulum swung back and forth counting the seconds. I read the time, it was half-past four. I was exhausted, yet looking through the glass, my nose pressed up to it like a child's, excited me. It kept me vigilant in the early hours of the morning.

To the left there was a chaise lounge and a door that had been left open. A dark bedroom was exposed. Dr. Remington had removed his clothing and was sleeping peacefully. I looked at Asha, she was also fast asleep. I boiled with anticipation at the thought of my task. Dr. Remington was vulnerable. The image filled me with hatred, excitement, and the desire to end him then and there.

I looked at Asha, it was odd the way her lips began to move. They twitched from side to side while she slept. She began to open and close her mouth. I watched intently. Asha's voice was higher than I had imagined it being. I had forgotten how young the child was. I listened in on the small sleeping girl for whatever conversation her dreams produced. I bent down next to her delicate breathing face. Small pockets of steam released from her mouth with each exhale. Steam enveloped small words until sentences came.

She spoke: Blum. Blum. Her body shuttered. It's very hot here.

I did not understand what she meant, but I did not wake her.

It is flaming. I cannot see you Blum, but I know you are there. You must be there.

I am here Asha, I whispered into her ear. I am here for you.

It is not the child that speaks, Blum. I recoiled from Asha, realizing whom the voice really belonged to.

Isabelle? I said quietly, wanting to believe so badly that I had made a connection with the dead.

Yes, Blum. It is I, she responded through the child.

Isabelle, it can't be true? Where are you?

My heart pounded ferociously in my chest. If I could have, I would have ripped the soul of the woman I loved from the body of that small child.

Blum, there is little time before he returns. Her voice was weak and hollow, it echoed from deep inside the child.

Who, Isabelle? Who is returning?

You must listen, Blum, the Midnight Man will soon return. He holds me here in limbo.

My intellect quieted my instinct to scream.

I have become the collateral for your foul bargain with the Midnight Man, Blum. He will hold me here until he knows you have delivered on your agreement. Blum, your quest for revenge has poisoned your mortal soul.

I leaned in closer to the girl. I do this for you, Isabelle.

I speak to you now to warn you of the danger he is trying to entangle you in.

Tell me, Isabelle. Tell me what it is I must know.

There is a curse, Blum. The curse is not one with which you were born, rather it is one that you may acquire. The Midnight Man would have you believe that you are the only viable successor to his corrupt throne.

I remained silent.

The contract you signed with that devil has tied your soul to the world of the dead. You have begun your metamorphosis. But, you have only started the rituals you must complete to become the demon that he is. There is still time to save yourself from his evil grasp.

Isabelle, I love you. I must save you from him. I don't care what happens to me. How can I save you, Isabelle? I want to protect you from this devil, the Midnight Man.

He has seen the possibility of your fate, Blum. In order to become him you will have to commit the heinous acts that will cement the curse. But, it is your choice to complete them. That is why he has brought you back to life, has encouraged you to seek revenge. He knows you have the potential to take his place, that you will stop at nothing to avenge my death.

I cannot bear to have you suffering under his tyranny. I must avenge you. He's evil, I screamed as I slammed my fists down on the grating.

Listen, you must not commit those heinous acts or you will be damned to share the fate he has held. Patricide, infanticide, suicide; you must know those are the acts that will corrupt your mortal soul.

Isabelle, don't leave me. I rocked my body next to that of the child.

Quiet, my love, she spoke, hushing my protests. He is watching. You must remember he is always watching. In the shadows he has a way to see. I must go, Blum.

Isabelle, I said as my tears began to drop onto Asha's face. Isabelle, I whispered, but there was no response from the sleeping babe, and I knew that Isabelle had gone. Isabelle's warning did nothing to soothe my mind. The Midnight Man is wrong about my fate. The doctor will pay for Isabelle's death and I will have my revenge, I whispered. She will be free.

After some time, I gathered myself and looked back inside at the man that had tortured my lover. I looked at the sleeping man that I desired to slaughter in every imaginable way. She had urged me to relinquish my quest, but the rage inside my mind spoke louder than ever before. I sat there for some time looking into the window, waiting for logic or passion to take hold.

I will not kill him in the light of this moon, in the wake of her words, I thought to myself. I must have time to consider what she has told me. Yet, even though she had warned me, I was certain that the doctor's death would not break any laws of humankind. I would free my love. It tortured me to think that she was his prisoner. I did not want to imagine the strange and terrible devices the Midnight Man might use on her.

I let my mind go and recalled the day she died, recalled the foul experiments the doctor had once performed on her. I begged with every inch of my soul that the Midnight Man would not repeat what Dr. Remington had done.

☺

Dawn spread itself over the city. The day of her execution had arrived. Small black birds perched themselves on wires, gutters, rooftops, and signs. A lone raven stood, like a black sentinel, on a large statue that marked the center of a nearby public square. Its black eyes focused on me, it cocked its head, let out a dry caw, and fluttered off into the morning sun. I had not slept. I had not eaten. I was exhausted and yet I did not crave the comforts of food or bed. It had been six months since her initial arrest. The Magistrates desired to have the child inside of her grow before her death. They wanted to pull on every cord of compassion I held. They knew that if my child was harmed they would have succeeded in breaking both my mind and spirit.

Though they searched tirelessly, they did not find me. I spent most of the time in abandoned buildings, always moving, never settling for too long, not communicating with anyone. I searched relentlessly for where they kept her, my captured Isabelle, but could not find her. My beard, long hair, and destitute appearance hid me well in a city filled with vagrants. Most of the time I hid in anger, and plotted how I might save Isabelle. I was absolutely powerless and that is exactly what the Magistrates desired.

I climbed down from my hiding place on a rooftop and ended up in a dark alley. I wanted to get a better view of the screens that the Magistrates kept focused on Isabelle's body both day and night. She was buckled down to a steel gurney. The Capital had witnessed, as the doctor had promised, her belly grow into that of a mother's. It would be a public execution, a slow and torturous one; one that they were hoping would draw me from my place of hiding in order to exchange my life for hers. The crowds filling the plaza were terrified, and yet they stood with their eyes transfixed on the girl that had struggled for months. She had been fed through funnels and tubes, unable to move or break free from her bonds.

From the entrance to the alley I looked up at the large screens spanning the circumference of the square. The High Magistrate flickered onto the screen. He smiled at the audience. The sight of his large nose, pimpled face, and yellow teeth sickened me. The High Magistrate's voice began to ring out. He spoke to the crowd of anxious and impatient onlookers.

It is not the plan of the Democracy, under the guidance and tutelage of the elected Magistrates, to lead the world into warfare. Quite to the contrary, it is our responsibility to defend ourselves from these ruthless dogs. The word *dogs* landed so gruffly, so bitterly, so thickly that he let out a long series of coughs from deep inside his chest. This one shall serve as an example to the remainder.

He resumed smoking his cigarette; its tip glowed red. The mark of three black dots formed a triangle on his robes. His hood, pulled back to reveal his wormy face, was so long it almost hung down to the floor. I looked away from the screens and hid in the crowd. I did not want to risk being spotted amongst the crowd and shot. I felt the need to get closer to Isabelle. I love her, I thought desperately.

Dr. Remington, it is time to begin, the High Magistrate said.

The screen flickered back to Isabelle. Her eyes opened to greet the on-looking crowd of long gray faces. Her gaze pierced deep into my chest. It sliced through my skin with precision, cracked my sternum, and found my heart. The blood pooled up inside me and for a moment my heart stopped, refused to beat, both congested and powerless, till her sweet and child-like smile jolted it and it began to beat again. She smiled for me, and I knew it. She smiled to tell me not to give myself up for her. She smiled until Dr. Remington took out his scalpel and began to run the blade shallowly over her exposed breasts. I could not watch. I closed my eyes and imagined that we were somewhere else.

Isabelle wore a crown of wildflowers mixed with shining golden wheat. The small yellow and purple buds that blended with the long, soft, feathered shafts spun around her head like a golden circlet set with precious stones. It complemented the way her sun-streaked hair flowed down over her bare shoulders. Her hair appeared to flow as if it were suspended in water. It moved, curled, folded upon itself in the current of hot air. It fanned out as if she were caught inside a flowing stream.

I heard her screams.

She passed through the tall grasses between us playing with the heads of wheat, letting the stalks slide through her fingers. Her fingers were soft. They caught the light of the afternoon sun, formed shadows on the stems. Occasionally she turned her head back to see if I was following. We looked at each other through the long, shimmering, undulating stems of wild grass. Her lips opened into a smile. She opened her arms and beckoned to me in the hot wind.

The crunching sound of bone.

I would have liked to take the girl right there in the long grass. She picked some wild flowers from the field and placed them into a bouquet that she held in her hand. I smiled back at her, chased after her in the fields. I outstretched my hand to touch her small palm. I placed her small hand in my larger one, and she grasped it like she had done before. She touched my hand as if she knew its every line, its every golden hair, and rough knuckle.

There was a gasp from the audience of horrified onlookers.

Her nails were beautiful. They were a vibrant red. You are beautiful, I said as I looked into her green eyes, which sparkled iridescently in the fading sunlight. In the light of the vanishing day she seemed angelic, ethereal, a sprite cast in the gold of the setting sun.

Her screaming broke my thoughts and I opened my eyes again.

They had positioned her upside-down, hanging from a steel girder. Her hair was wrapped in a large piece of twisting gauze. She bared resemblance to a woman of the Orient wreathed in white silk. She had been lathered with resin and tubes had been placed in the incisions the doctor had made. I watched as they drained the blood out of her body.

In the bright, neon lights of the room, the color of her beautiful skin was tarnished by the long lines of caramel liquid dripping down her slender frame. Her whole body was the color of egg yolks left out to dry. Yet, she was still beautiful. She was a precious piece of polished amber suspended from a necklace crafted of steel.

To the onlookers she was one of the barbarians from the west. Too burnt from the sun, crusted over with filth from windstorms, and dressed in the clothes of nature. They saw all of her; she was exposed for the crowds. They gawked at her. When I had imagined making love to her in the fields, amongst the wildflowers, it had not been in this way. I did not wish to share her with the men who walked the plaza, the women who gasped in terror. Their eyes watched her red lips colored in iron dust, her tan skin turned a coddled yellow, her sex dyed a deep purple. Her sex was not the light pink that I had once seen. It was not the soft womb that had taken me inside of it, not the place where I had felt the pleasure of creating our unborn child. The sight of her sex gave me no pleasure. There was no thrill in her exposure, no thrill in seeing her womanhood. She was, in the light, in the gleaming fluorescence, anatomical, a piece of meat hung on a silver hook.

She was deliberately exposed, stripped of all her dignity, and I wished for nothing more than to protect her from their peering eyes. I felt her embarrassment and pain. Her breasts hung awkwardly towards her clavicle, like two lumps of flesh trying to drip down to the floor, like melted lard falling into a crackling fire. If she had been lactating her breasts would have created stalagmites on the white tiled floor. I wondered in that moment if the cream of her breasts would have calcified on the ground, warped, changed with age, grown over the years, until she was completely covered in a column of bone. I looked at her, a caryatid in the making, and in her flickering green eyes I saw defeat. I felt the anger begin to boil in me. I began to wring my hands. I felt my voice aching to scream out at the crowd. I wanted to burst their eardrums with my booming voice, but instead I was silent.

Dr. Remington continued to work her over. Pieces of broken bone poked through her emaciated skin. She had become shriveled and twisted; her spine a small dying tree with branches of bone where ribs should have been. They extended off of the trunk of her spine like curling twigs with no leaves. I gazed upon the flesh of my lover inverted directly upon itself. Her screams resonated in the plaza as Dr. Remington took much joy in twisting her innards out for all of us to see. He destroyed her every human feature, the form of her womanhood, her once beautiful face. Her green eyes hung sorrowfully with the last vestiges of life, glass paperweights, filled to the edge with clear bubbles of air, frozen solid in glass.

Dr. Remington hummed to himself gleefully as he dismantled her body. He sang the national anthem. He seemed to delight in stabbing her in the chest and opening her up like she had once done to him. I recalled the blade sticking out of the doctor's chest, if only she had twisted it harder.

My breathing quickened and sweat began to moisten the skin underneath my clothes. My palms were clammy. The nervous tension building inside of my veins traveled from organ to organ, shook each one individually: liver, kidney, intestine, lungs, heart, and brain. I felt each unravel itself and then congeal, each turn to acidic liquid and then reform inside. The urge to release the contents of my stomach grew, but I did not, would not allow myself the relief. Such an action would have been disrespectful to Isabelle. I could not allow myself to dishonor the tortured body of the woman I loved so deeply. I knew that when the Black Boots caught up with me, I would end my days the same as her.

It was over faster than I could have imagined. Dr. Remington had removed the unborn babe from her womb and it was taken away. I looked away. I could not bear to see the child we had created, so savagely torn from her body. I did not want to think of the tortures they conjured up for our babe, in the adjacent room.

Isabelle's body had become an empty shell. The beautiful butterfly was removed from the brown carapace. Isabelle had become the cast off detritus of a cocoon, the casing of the bug rotting and not the brilliant colors of its wings taking flight into the sky. I imagined hearing her raspy voice one last time. The power of it sparked a change within me, a flood, an outpouring of tears.

Goodbye, Blum, she said.

Stop, I screamed from the pavilion. The crowds moved quickly away from me, surrounded me in an inescapable circle. Stop, I screamed. Kill me instead. I am Blum, I am Blum. Kill me instead, I yelled towards the screens, towards the image of my one love, but God did not hear me.

I will kill you, I said as the tears streamed down my face and the Black Boots carried me screaming from the crowd. I figured it would only be a matter of time until my death. I did not care. I wished for death, but death did not come. Instead, I was confined to the metal cell that became my prison and my home, until I was cast out into the wasteland.

The last of the memories we shared had unfolded inside my head, splashed onto the screen of my mind a final time.

V

Asha rose, came to my side, and pulled at my shirt. At first I did not recognize her, she was blue with cold from the morning frost, a double of Isabelle's dead body on the doctor's metal slab.

I'm hungry, she whispered. Asha motioned to her mouth with her small fingers. The child had spoken. We had little food left.

I felt close to Asha. In my mind she would replace the unborn baby they withdrew from my lover's womb. I knew for certain that Asha held some deep connection to the twisted fate the Midnight Man was spinning for my soul. I gave her the remaining food I had and she ate it in silence.

I peered into the doctor's apartment from my perch. I needed to study his every movement, it was the only way I could formulate the perfect moment to strike. I imagined that Dr. Remington must have had many homes throughout the city, many apartments, offices, and halls for his use. Though small, this space felt regal. The golden clock told the time, half past ten. Dr. Remington came out of his bedroom fully dressed. He wore a pressed black suit. I watched as he sat and began to read a book he pulled from the shelf.

It did not take long for the small pale man to enter the room and sit in one of the chairs facing the doctor. I cleaned a tiny bit of soot off the window so I could see better. They could not see me. The other man was old, his face was wrinkled, but in youth he could have been quite attractive. His left eye twitched uncontrollably in intermittent fits. I watched the two men for a long time before realizing that a small vent next to the window would allow me to listen in on their conversation.

How does it make you feel to be here right now, Frank? The doctor asked the man who was shaking his foot and twisting his fingers into knots. I could not keep from looking at his twitching eye, it was gray, like his hair.

My brother brought me here today, doctor. He found me at home and reminded me it was time to see you.

A pause, Dr. Remington wrote some notes on a pad of paper. His face was stoic. Yes, I understand, he said. How do you feel right now, Frank? A pause. I looked at the pendulum on the grandfather clock. It swung back and forth in a steady stream of motion.

I feel nervous, doctor. Yes, I feel nervous, his voice quavered. I feel like time is running out. I'm afraid to be here right now.

Well, Frank, it's okay to feel afraid. We are all human and we all get scared. He had a deep voice. Fear is natural. It's your anxiety, Frank, that lets your fear get out of control. Your obsessions are all part of your anxiety. Now tell me what you are afraid of, Frank.

A pause, four seconds, four golden flashes of the pendulum. I am afraid to die, doctor. A pause, four seconds. Dr. Remington wrote some more notes.

Right Frank, that is all we have time for today. Continue taking 40mg of Ryxolene and I will see you next week at the same time. Until then, visit with my research assistant, Dr. Barton. He will fill your prescription. A pause, four seconds, four more swings.

Thank you doctor, he said as he stood up.

Dr. Remington got up and opened the door for him. He closed it behind his patient and then sat down and wrote some final notes on the pad. Dr. Remington read for a while and then left the apartment.

Asha rested at my feet, closed her eyes in the morning gloom. The clock's swinging plumb rocked back and forth, as though it was rocking her to sleep.

The appointment seemed routine. It appeared as though the doctor actually cared to help his patient. He did not resemble the demon that had slaughtered Isabelle.

I went down into the alley in search of something to pry the window open with. I jumped into one of the dumpsters and tore ferociously at the trash until I found a long piece of discarded iron. It was black, rusted, long, thin, and it would do. I crawled back up and jammed the bar of metal between the corroded window and its even more corroded sill. I applied pressure to the rod and with some work I forced the window open.

I stepped inside the room. I longed for my chance to pay him back for what he had done to Isabelle. I could smell him everywhere. It was the same sick scent that clung to Isabelle after he had been with her in Jex's den. The office smelled of old books. It was warm. I shut the window lightly so that the heat would not escape. Asha remained outside.

I walked into Dr. Remington's bedroom. It smelled like sweat. His bed was still warm. My heart was pounding. I did not know if he was going to return, if he would find me there. I felt as though my body might catch on fire from the rage that I was experiencing. I believed my body might combust from desire, that my own bloodlust might erupt in brilliant scarlet flames.

I went into his bathroom. A dirty towel was tossed on the floor. The faucet dripped. The mirror was old and cracked. The beauty of the place had been lost to the war. I looked in the mirror and saw my reflection divided in the broken shards. My mouth, spread open in a grin, was split a hundred times over, teeth upon teeth. A shark's mouth reflected back at me.

I closed my eyes and then opened them again. I looked at the shower and imagined Isabelle standing in it. I imagined the room filling with the steam from underground pipes.

Isabelle stood beside me. She was nude. The steam from the shower filled the room. A strange white fog blurred my vision. Isabelle, her long wet hair stuck to her skin, stood before me. Her nails were red. I moved forward to kiss the nape of her neck. Something pulled her backwards away from me. My hands reached out to grab her, yet she was just out of reach. Not a word came from the ghost that stood before me.

Isabelle, I said quietly, but then she was gone, a fractured memory expended in my brain. After a moment I could no longer see her naked form. My heart fluttered as the fog continued to rise. She was gone, lost inside the clouds of mist.

I heard something jangling the locks of the main entryway. I grabbed the iron bar, snuck into the closet, and closed the door. I stood there quietly, smelled his clothes, his scent. It made me sick.

Hushed voices, quiet voices, I could not recognize the voices at first. His voice was deep. It was dark in the closet. The other voice was that of a woman, a younger woman's voice. I have heard that voice before. It sounded like Isabelle, a woman in her youth. I smelled cigarettes and then Orange-Labyrinth.

I had left Asha outside. I recalled her small blue face. Why did I leave her alone? I thought. I heard something fall onto the bed. I heard the sound of kissing, of bodies entwining. I started to smell liquor, sweat, and sex. I was disgusted by the man's every action. I felt anger rising inside of me.

I listened to the moans of that drunken whore. Fuck me, doctor, she wailed.

My hands balled into tight fists. My nails dug so deeply into my palms that they drew blood. My insides were twisting as I remembered the way he had entered Isabelle.

Dr. Remington, Dr. Remington, the whore repeated faster, time and time again. Her words became more and more frenzied, until she loosed a scream so pronounced, so animalistic, so primal, that I felt my own sex enlarge.

I could not wait any longer. I held the iron bar tightly in my hand. Rust leeched into the wounds my nails had dug into my palms. I heard the clock in the other room strike the twelfth hour. It tolled twelve solid strikes as its pendulum swung back and forth. I smashed the doctor alongside his head and his naked body crashed to the floor.

However, my hands, like the golden pendulum, could not be stopped. I landed eleven blows into the young whore. I splashed blood and chunks of her womanly curves onto his white sheets. The whore was dead. She was a girl no older than sixteen.

I tied Dr. Remington's body to the base of the bathroom sink. I used a combination of belts and twine I found in his closet. A large scar covered the place where Isabelle had once wounded him. The ridges of his scar, lit in the bright bathroom lights, resembled a mountain range illuminated by the hot sun.

I lit a cigarette from his pack and slapped his face until he regained consciousness.

Dr. Remington. Are you afraid? I whispered to him.

He nodded groggily.

It's okay to feel afraid. We are all human and we all get scared. I blew smoke out of my mouth and it wrapped around his face. Fear is natural. I paused and looked at his shivering, pathetic figure. I paused and took a drag of the cigarette. Now tell me what you are afraid of? I grinned as smoke poured out between my teeth.

I am afraid to die, he said. His hazel eyes shown as large as dimes in the fluorescent light. I watched him as he tried to free himself.

What do you want with me, Blum? He stuttered.

I continued to smoke my cigarette and downed a Z-Pam.

What are you taking? He asked.

He was afraid, so very afraid. His vulnerability enchanted me.

My patients will come for me today. They'll see what you've done, you monster. He slipped on the words like he was slipping on wet marble.

Monster? I am no monster. You are the monster. I looked over at the whore. A little young for you Dr. Remington, don't you think?

He trembled and tried to wrench himself free.

Let me go. I don't want to die. I don't want to die like this, he pleaded. Desperate words issued from his mouth, they tasted delicious as I swallowed them whole. In that moment, with the strike of the golden pendulum, I was the one in control. I grinned. Dr. Remington began to sob, his tears came down in sheets.

Don't cry now. I'll be right back. In the mean time you can calm down and get some rest before I begin.

Begin? He screamed.

Well yes, doctor, you did not think I would make your death quick, did you?

I touched his face and wiped away his tears. He tried to bite my finger, but I pulled back and wagged it from side to side in front of his face.

Don't do that, Dr. Remington. It's really quite unattractive, I said sarcastically.

I took a towel and placed it in his mouth, tied it in place with a piece of cord. Some gasps and screams escaped from him but they did not penetrate the building's thick walls. Outside, the Capital was filled with the hum of traffic and the rattling of trains. The Capital was filled with the screams of mothers, the sound of gunfire, and the moans of erotic pleasure escaping from behind closed doors.

His feet were tied, which rendered him helpless. I figured I could leave him alone and he would be fine. He would be forced to just wait there on the floor for my return.

I will return, I said to him.

I went to the windowsill and woke Asha. I carried her into the building.

Do not go in that room Asha, I instructed her.

Her sleepy eyes, still groggy, did not pay any attention to my blood-soaked clothes. You are not to go into the back room. Do you understand me?

She nodded her head.

Good, sweet girl. I love you. The words came so naturally, so willingly, to my lips. I liked saying those words. We will be staying here for a while. The doctor is an old friend of mine. It is okay for us to stay here.

I laid her down on the chaise lounge, covered her with a blanket, and she fell peacefully back to sleep. I watched her sleep for a moment and stroked her soft hair. Such a vision, surely an incarnation of the woman I love, I thought to myself. I kissed Asha lightly on her cheek.

I went to the main door and placed a sign on it that read: ALL APPOINTMENTS CANCELLED. I stepped into the bedroom. I was swallowed in darkness. I shut the door behind me.

VI

The skin on Dr. Remington's face felt like kid gloves, clean-shaven, smooth, buttery. I slid my hand up and down his cheek. He held his eyes closed tightly; small tears welled up in them. It was then that I noticed the small lines that extended from the corners of his lids. I had not seen the wrinkles before, had not seen them through the wall of confidence he had projected. It was not until that moment of defeat and submission, that I saw the real man. The man before me, as striking as he was, was at least twenty years my senior. I looked into Dr. Remington's face. He could not scream and thus would not foil the silence of the moment, the transient peace I had created.

I spoke: Do you know much of anatomy, Dr. Remington?

He nodded.

Well of course you do. You are a physician. I learned much about human anatomy when I was a Black Boot. At night, I used to watch my commander practice his combat skills. He always had a large glass of dark-brown liquor in his hand. He used sword, knife, and bayonet to show me the most efficient ways to kill a man. He showed me how to render a man utterly useless with just one stab, slash, or cut.

I paused and looked down at the scars on my forearm. I held my arm out so that he could see. This is what I use knives for, I said. You see, my commander and I were made of different stuff. He was a fighter. It shaped his career, shaped his ambition, his need for control, his arrogance. It shaped his aggression, nursed it like a calf at its mothers tit. I laughed to myself.

He once told me the best way to debilitate a man is to strike for his eyes. Even a light punch into the eye will render a man dazed, a knife blind. Without much more work, a few fell swoops into the neck or belly, he would be dead.

I motioned as I spoke, lunging to and fro, practicing my thrusts with an imaginary blade. I stopped and looked at him, enjoyed the power I held over him. I stooped down to his level, picked his chin up. He breathed heavily. He forced air in and out of his flaring nostrils.

Yes, I know much about the anatomy of men. I can look at a man and tell if he is meek or self-assured with one glance. I can determine if he is rich or poor; if he treats his wife and family well, or if he is a fool, a prince, or a peasant. There is much skill in observation, in noticing the small details of a man. Even the scent of a man can tell you his constitution. I am grateful to my commander for teaching me to be observant, to dissect the body, the man, to discern the very memories of his past by observing his movement, his gait, the way he holds his hands, the sound of his voice, whether it is thick with pride or thin with reservation.

Through the years I have been able to perfect this skill. I can tell much about a man with a quick glance into his eyes. A man's eyes are his most vulnerable spot, the brain's connection to the outside world. Dr. Remington, you are keeping secrets behind those eyes of yours. I stared at him, his heart pounded feverishly in his chest.

The body is a beautiful creation, a machine, an anatomical sculpture. I have always revered the body, admired its grace and beauty. I stood up again and paced the room. Isabelle was beautiful, don't you agree? My voice tensed. Did you enjoy murdering her? I let the question dangle in the air, let it swing back and forth like the golden pendulum that kept the time in the other room.

I bent down and carefully removed Dr. Remington's gag and waited for his reply. He looked down at the floor, contemplating whether or not he should scream for help. I turned on the water in the shower, to muffle the sounds he might utter. I was excited, and understood how the intimacy of the moment might at any second break through him and release itself in the form of an orgasmic scream.

It would be unwise to try and make a commotion, Dr. Remington. After all, you know as well as I do, screams are common in the night. In these times, only fools try to come to the aid of others.

He opened his mouth, and I saw the pink of his spongy tongue. I wanted to cut it out, but refrained from doing so, knowing that there would be time for that in the future.

He spoke: Blum, you do not know everything. I had no choice in the matter of your Isabelle.

There is always a choice, doctor, I said as I picked some of the whore's blood out from under my fingernails. You had a choice when you decided to cut her in two, did you not?

You know as well as I do that there is no disobeying the Magistrates. It is the High Magistrate that you should hunt, not me. You do not know what it is you are about to do. You still have a choice, Blum. Turn back and leave me.

No, I said defiantly. He hung his head down and waved it from side to side.

You are a foolish traitor, Blum. A failure. You refuse to submit to authority and that is why you wish to destroy the paradise we have created.

Paradise, I said. This is no paradise, doctor.

Dr. Remington continued to speak: Blum, your need for control and power is just as wicked as the Magistrates'. You are more similar to them than you would like to believe. A moment of silence elapsed. Your need for power and control stems from your insecurity, your past, the lack of a father figure.

A pause.

Do you know much about your father, Blum?

I don't have a father. I never had a father, I said with hatred in my voice. I was raised in an orphanage. I was forced to fight for the Magistrates in their unjust crusades.

I am sorry, Blum. That must have been difficult for a young child.

My face turned sour and I curled my lip at his feigned sympathy. I kicked him in the ribs and he doubled over.

I turned around and walked over to the window. I could barely make out the shapes of the city through the thick layer of soot covering the glass. I looked at the mess of carnage on the bed. As despicable as it was, I did not regret the whore's death. Her dark blood pooled onto the white sheets and dripped onto the floor.

I rolled the body of the dead woman in the white bed linens. Dr. Remington turned away as I packaged her body into a neat parcel. In death she was much smaller, much more delicate. The smell coming off of her body was repulsive. Her odor was akin to rotting meat or raw eggs spoiled in the sun. I gagged as I took her body to the window. I placed her body on the windowsill and retrieved the iron rod from beside the bed. After prying open the bedroom window, I shoved her body onto the fire escape lining the building. I shut the window. A flock of crows flew over to her decomposing corpse. The golden pendulum ticked onward in the neighboring room.

Why question me about my father? I shouted as I turned around to face him.

My curiosity was building, I felt like I was going to explode. I started moving closer to him, my fists balled tightly by my sides. Dr. Remington recoiled, his muscles tightened, he had not expected such an outburst, such an upsurge in emotion. His face seemed in control, but his eyes told me that he feared for his life.

The place smelled like a charnel house, a butcher shop, from the remnants of that putrid whore. I smelled her fluid, her sex, her smells of womanhood. I grabbed a few pills from my pocket and swallowed them with the saliva in my mouth. The Z-Pam, bittersweet, chalky, melted down my throat, coated my stomach, and entered my bloodstream. A refreshing coolness overtook me and I felt utterly placid, languid, as I slithered closer to the dark man who tried to wriggle himself free from his bindings. I, like a snake circling and closing in on its prey, moved from side to side, hemming him in, making his world as small as he had made mine.

Do you know my father, Dr. Remington? I asked him firmly. He looked shocked, as if I had plucked a chord inside of him, so deep and intrinsic that it sent reverberations throughout his body.

Blum, you do not know what you are doing. Turn back. His breathing was rapid, his eyes bugged out as if he knew I could tell he was holding something from me.

Speak, I held the iron bar to his throat.

He spoke: Your father is a true visionary, Blum.

You know my father? My words burst violently from my throat.

He appeals to the Magistrates' desire for control, he appeals to their quest for perfection, for genius, for submission.

His smile was haunting. For a moment I thought he would evaporate as the Midnight Man had done before, into the shadow and the mist.

It was your father's science that made all of this possible, the world we live in, our utopia, Dr. Remington said.

Utopia? This is hell. I pushed the bar harder into his neck.

Call it what you will, Blum, but if it were not for your father's research the Magistrate's grand solution would never have succeeded. He understood that with action comes power, with power comes fear, with fear comes control. He understood that to take control, others would need to be subdued. He understood that there was no room in our society for their kind. He understood that the Jookies' impurity was tainting the lineage that the Magistrates were trying to preserve. Those who were unfit for labor would be evacuated, those who were strong would work in the steel quarry. It was quite simple, neat, clean, organized. He knew that the citizens would be easily controlled if they were given the Offering.

Dr. Remington laughed until I knocked him across the face with the bar. The hit did not draw blood, but crunched loudly upon impact.

He turned his eyes towards the floor like an injured animal.

Your father's dream has become reality. Yet, his dream did not end there. His vision included a future where there would be no one to challenge the Magistrates' rule. He desired the Overmen, a race of soldiers that would be subservient, controllable, obedient. Clean of memory, of pain, of history, of time. The Overmen would know nothing but the commands that God delivers through the Magistrates. They would be pure.

You speak only lies. They told me my father died in the war, I said. I hit him once more with the bar leaving a large bloody gash.

No, you are wrong, Blum. There is so much you do not understand about the nature of your reality. The words recalled the exact phrase the Midnight Man had once spoken to me.

There is a connection, there is resolution in what I say. You are foolish to think that by killing me you will stop what has already been set into motion, has already been planned. I believe you are too late, Blum. He laughed haughtily. It was a strange reaction from a man that had been exposed to my volatile wrath.

Yes, Dr. Remington, I may be too late, but you must remember it is still I who holds the power to make you suffer. He stopped smiling.

Then go ahead and kill me, Blum.

I thought silently for a second, my hands clutched the weapon tightly. There was no mercy for Isabelle, I screamed as I landed a severe blow to his chest. I stabbed him in the very spot where Isabelle had once wounded him. Fresh blood spouted from the old scar.

I will kill you, Dr. Remington, there is no doubt of that.

I felt happiness wash over me, like the first rain after a dry summer.

The sick satisfaction that I would be the very last person to enter him, the last to smell his blood and bones, to massage his muscles inside and out, as he had done to my Isabelle.

You are a fool, Blum, he screamed at me. You are a pathetic fool. You are cursed. I kicked Dr. Remington's head into the pedestal sink and his nose cracked. Blood ran freely from the fracture on his face.

It's too late for your cause, Blum, Dr. Remington said through the blood and the mucus that poured out of him. My death will not undo the Democracy.

I took the iron bar and jammed it deep into Dr. Remington's leg. Nothing fatal, but the crunching noise and the string of sobs that followed pleased me. It let me know the extent of his excruciating pain.

The child lives, Blum. I stopped digging into him.

No, that cannot be.

It is true, Blum. The child still lives. I could not kill her, she is my own flesh and blood. I could not do it.

What do you mean your own flesh and blood? The child was yours? I lifted the sharp rod and pierced him through the stomach.

Blum, the child is yours. I sent her to live in the streets. His words failed as more blood poured out of him. I could not kill my granddaughter. Will you kill me now, Blum? Your own father.

I do not believe the poisonous words you speak. I saw you with Isabelle. I saw her pleasure you. It made me sick.

Dr. Remington looked sullen for a moment. I slept with Isabelle, yet the child cannot be mine.

Why do you tell me this? How do you know the child is not yours? I am no longer fertile, Blum. He choked on his saliva. I have been unable to impregnate a woman since your whore of a mother. The disease she left me with caused my infertility. Her pestilence, her tarnished womanhood, left me barely a man.

I listened intently, realizing the gravity of what he spoke to me.

The only future I have is in my genetic research. When I discovered my infertility I had to, he paused to hack up some blood. I had to reconsider who would carry on my line. You are my son. You are the last of my seed. You and my granddaughter are all I have left. Yet, I never desired to leave behind a whore's son. I never desired to leave you my great legacy.

I do not desire your legacy, I screamed wildly at the man.

We looked into each other's eyes. A current of electricity passed between us. I felt Isabelle's ghost standing there beside me. His arrogant smile returned.

Your mother was a whore, Blum. You are nothing but the bastard child of a whore. I did not wish to call you my son. Nonetheless, you are my son. You are a part of me.

I do not trust the words you speak, you devil, I shouted as I put my hands to my head.

What I speak is true, Blum, he said, gaining confidence. It is but a matter of time before the Black Boots come for me. They are most likely already on their way. They will be here soon enough. He laughed through the blood and the pain.

Isabelle's ghost ached to be set free.

Do it Blum, finish him, I heard the Midnight Man whisper from behind me.

My voice rose to a feverish pitch. My father's dying body started to shake uncontrollably. Urine leaked down his leg. I heard the pendulum swinging in the other room.

There will be no mercy, I thought to myself. I felt Isabelle's ghost guide my hand holding the bar high into the air. Dr. Remington cringed. He closed his eyes in an effort to try and disappear. With the remainder of his energy he violently thrashed about and knocked himself into the porcelain of the pedestal sink. The floor vibrated from his spasms.

The critical seconds that held the weapon suspended in the air seemed infinite. Isabelle's blood cried out to me for vengeance. The ticking of that shining golden pendulum was all I heard.

The moment had come. Far away the angel of death sounded a great horn. The beat of hooves rapidly approached from a distance. The buzzing of flies, the laughter of the Midnight Man, the echoes of deep sonorous groans filled my ears. I plunged the bar deep into his belly and dragged it up slowly so that he could feel the burning pain. I pulled it out and went back for more, dug deeper and deeper, through intestine, chest, heart, and brain. I felt his life escaping through his muffled screams of agony.

You will never be my father, I raged. I pounded the metal into his broken ribs time and time again.

A smile as wide as the night sky spanned across my face. The downward hacks landed into bone. He felt the bite of iron into cartilage, sinew, and gut. I loosed a scream so piercing and high that I thought the mirrored glass would shatter about my blurred form. Isabelle cried through me. Her cry of vengeance reached the ceiling, escaped through pipe and shaft, expelled into the night air.

A rage of combat consumed me. My head felt like it might burst into a conflagration, a holocaust of the mind. My clothes were soaked in him; his insides were now exposed like the whore I had killed before. I dropped the bar, and still I clawed at him with my bare hands, tearing flesh from bone. In a violent burst, I dug my hand into his eye socket and retrieved the eyeball that had mocked me only moments before. I tossed it to my side and resumed my demonic feast.

His blood ran like mercury upon the tiled floor, it spilled around me like golden sap, like streams of pure ruby reflecting the morning sun. It smelled like metal, iron shards, rust. I lifted my hands to the air as I felt the inferno completely consume me.

I stepped away from the puddle of man before me. I untied him and threw his corpse into the tub. I plugged the drain and watched as his blood pooled about him. The water surrounding him was warm, stained the color of rust. I turned the running water off and crouched beside him. I held the bar soaked in his blood in front of my eyes. I smiled. I saw my reflection through the red sap that ran down its shaft and dripped onto the tiled floor.

They will certainly come for me soon, I thought. In the moment, I did not care. As steam rose from the bath, my lungs filled with warm wet air. A cherry mist clouded the room. His body was tranquil in the hot swampy water; it was swollen, bloated, like Isabelle's had been. He was still. I felt as though I had just entered the world anew, a newborn exiting the womb, covered in the crust of its mother's interior. A calm, a silence, a pure fluorescent white cloaked the world. My mind was empty of thought and emotion, vacuous, nerves as still as the face of a glass, the face of a clock. My thoughts no longer spiraled, repeated, cycled, or churned like a great whirlpool.

I stroked him, held his hand in mine, and touched his dead face. In his face I saw myself. In that moment I loved the man. He looked so innocent. The holes that punctured his white skin ran deep. I placed my hand in the warm water and swirled it about creating tide pools dyed a rich shade of burgundy. The water felt soothing to my hand. His face, still as a windless day inside a hot valley of white grasses, seemed peaceful, at rest. It mirrored my cathartic state.

I closed my eyes and saw Isabelle.

Isabelle, it's time. You've been sleeping long enough.

No response.

Isabelle, why won't you speak to me? I wish you would speak to me. I hung my head low and placed it on my father's wet shoulder. I understand, I said, utterly defeated. I love you, I said as I placed my lips on his moist cheek. I stroked his head as I continued to dream of the girl, my Isabelle. I imagined her beside me, nude inside the white basin, my hands stroking her limp and lifeless body.

I heard whimpering behind me. I whipped around, and a spray of vibrant fluorescent pink doused Asha from the whites of her eyes to her boney ankles. Asha sat shivering behind me. She stared down at the eyeball beside her on the bathroom floor. Her mouth opened wide, she shook violently not knowing whether to run or embrace me. She was caught between the force for survival and the need for affection. Her green eyes glowed eerily in the brightness of the fluorescent tubes. The girl was covered in a fine scarlet mist, like fresh graffiti sprayed on a brick wall. Her clothes and her skin glistened as her limbs trembled inside of her young body.

Asha, she had seen it all. She wept, but did not move. I advanced slowly toward her. The guts that had once been inside of my father's body had been torn from his mutilated cadaver and were spread about the room.

I told you not to come in here, Asha.

There was no response, only silence. The Black Boots would be coming soon. I grabbed the child by her wrist.

Let go of me, she said as she struggled to break free.

Asha, you do not understand. This man, this, I pointed at him, thing. He was evil. You must understand; I will never hurt you.

I heard the Midnight Man through the mist. Your life is cursed, Blum. Yours is a life filled with death. Look around you now. Your father's blood surrounds you on the floor. The Midnight Man let out a peal of laughter that filled the small bathroom.

You knew of this, you devil. You knew I would seek revenge on my own father.

I lifted Asha up, she fought me, but I held her tightly and ran from Dr. Remington's apartment and the bathroom's fluorescent lights.

You cannot escape me, Blum. You cannot escape your fate. Through the darkness I can see you. I will follow you.

I looked down at Asha. Could she be my daughter, our daughter? I thought. When I looked away from her I noticed my vision had changed, it had blurred. It seemed as though logic had been inverted.

A vast hallway of doors was before me. I cradled the child in my arms and flew down the damp corridor. It felt as though the fabric of reality was being stretched, thinned, made translucent, as I raced against the pull of its strengthening riptide.

A draft pushed at us as I ran down the stairs. It smelled like death. We passed rooms on either side of the hallway that branched and broke free into more rooms, more corridors. The beating of that infernal golden clock resonated inside my ears. As I raced onward, I took note of my bloodstained hands. The red had coated me; it was indelible.

I quickened my pace as the smells grew stronger. Asha's face grew thin and pale. It was fading away, as if at any moment I would look down and no longer have her in my arms. I raced through the darkened hallways and dilapidated rooms.

Faster, I screamed to drive myself onward. Faster, faster, run faster, my voice blared violently into the nightmare that wrapped itself around my blood-drenched form.

I turned the corner. I still held the girl inside my arms. My muscles burned, but I pulled strength from my vast desire to keep her there with me. I was halted by that man hidden in shadow.

I stopped abruptly and pressed Asha tightly to my heaving chest. My embrace protected her. My breath raced violently out of control. My lungs were barely able to suck in the cold damp air. Still that smell, which began to reek of tar and grease, grew around us. The Midnight Man, as calm as ever, held Asha's dead rabbit in his hands. He stroked it slowly with his glove, as flies and maggots ate of the place where its tongue poured out of its frail body. He pressed it against his black suit, mirrored my embrace of the small child I held in my arms. The hallway smelled like a butcher shop, the stink of a mortuary. I heard the buzzing of insects and the call of black birds issuing from the darkness.

From the shadows I heard the Midnight Man say: The eve of our agreement draws to a close, Blum.

In that moment I recalled the people I had sent to their deaths: the Black Boots, the whores, even Zarian and Jex. My father's dead body lay bloated and butchered inside a bathtub. They no longer breathed, no longer felt the pulse of blood inside their veins. Their spirits had been washed out to sea. He would hold them there, until it was time to thread them once again into the current of his unending game.

Blum, look where your obsession and desire have led you, he spoke. His words echoed down the hall in the cold blackness. It is only a matter of time before the acts that you have committed against man shall condemn you to the curse that I bear. I will be free, and you my friend, will be a prisoner to these black wastes.

He laughed as I worked myself through the shadows that he cast. Your Isabelle might once again be free, but you Blum, will be mine forever. We stumbled forward in the dark as I held onto Asha as tightly as I could.

I cannot see, Asha screamed.

I tripped and fell. The world around us vanished, faded away to the sound of rushing water.

I woke up on a bridge, which spanned the river that snaked its way through the center of the Capital. The faint light of dawn was upon us; the city was quiet. We were covered in small flakes of ash that had blown in from the desert.

I held onto Asha tightly, so that she would not budge, so that she would be mine, so that we would be together forever. I cannot lose her now, my last vestige of Isabelle. I cannot bear to be truly alone, I thought. I feared whatever hellfire and damnation awaited me if I should succumb to the curse the Midnight Man so happily goaded me towards.

I took the child by her shoulders and looked into her shivering face. I love you, Asha, I whispered as I stared into her green eyes. Tears filled my eyes. I could tell that she did not know what to make of the words I had spoken to her. Though her heart yearned for affection, she knew how quickly my affection could turn into rage.

I love you, I repeated desperately. I know that I am not worthy of being your father, but you must trust me. I looked into her eyes, read them. I will find a way for us to be safe, Asha. I promise you that. I will find a way.

She did not try to free herself from my grasp. Inside I could tell that she was trying to find the courage to believe the words I had uttered.

Asha's small mouth barely made a noise when she spoke: You saved me once before. Her head dropped to my shoulder and her arms wrapped around my torso. I love you, she whispered as she clung to me.

The freezing cold water churned some thirty feet below the bridge. Her fear had been supplanted by a quiet peace. I looked at her soft face; a precious porcelain doll stared back at me. I felt safe with her; she gave me a renewed purpose, my life had been resurrected from Isabelle's ashes.

I will never hurt you, Asha, I said. In that moment, my desire for revenge had completely fallen away. It was as if the child had somehow siphoned the hatred from my bones. The moment had finally arrived. I began to feel peace of mind work its way through the synapses of my brain. I felt a freedom from the obsession that had plagued me for so many years. I realized that the child's life had superseded that of my own.

The knife cut into my back. Like a swarm of black angels, they descended upon us. I threw myself over Asha to protect her, but the

Black Boots pulled me away. I was stripped naked. I felt as Isabelle must have felt as she layed on Dr. Remington's table, ashamed and writhing in pain. They bound my body in leather straps. I gritted my teeth as they tied me up. Ash fell from the gray morning sky and covered my nude body. The water rushed below the bridge.

As I screamed and thrashed about, I saw the child being lifted above them. Before they tied the sack over my head, I caught a reflection in the water. Isabelle peered up at me from beneath the current.

Do not let her die, she mouthed up at me.

The Black Boot devils hoisted me over their shoulders and the deep laughter of the Midnight Man blended with the sound of my falling tears. Hoisted over their heads, I was carried into the city. I heard the ghosts of children playing and rolling amongst the ash, making snow angels in the delicate crystals that coated the boulevards.

VII

I awoke from my unconsciousness on the cold floor of what I imagined was an underground catacomb.

Don't try and fight me, a man's voice both low and guttural shouted from behind.

I tried to free myself, but I could not escape the leather straps that still held my arms behind my back. Through the burlap sack covering my head, I smelled ash and smoke being expelled from great smoke-stacks.

I continued to struggle in my bonds. The man dug his long gun into my spine, poked me with its metal tip.

Where is Asha? I screamed, but he did not reply.

In the moment, I wished that he would pull the trigger and end my misery and pain. After some time, the Black Boot pushed me forward and I fell into a hole. The fall did not break me; I landed in a pile of foul smelling straw. It was damp and cold. Another guard pulled me to my feet and pushed me forward. I could not see anything; it was completely black. I was somewhere under the streets of the city. I tried to get a sense of my surroundings, but it was hopeless. I heard voices and felt bodies. I bumped into corpses and maneuvered away from the groans of dying men. One man shuddered with fear when I ran into him.

Who is there? I whispered. He only spoke nonsense in return.

I felt my way around, running into other huddled figures. We were packed into the room very tightly. I felt a push from behind and almost fell over. I recovered myself and tried to make sense of the situation.

To the left, the Black Boots spoke in unison over the loudspeaker playing the anthem.

I followed the current of the horde. Am I dead? I wondered. I can only hope Isabelle is here with me amongst the dead I amble with. I heard the sound of large doors opening. The sack was pulled off of my head. The doors crashed closed behind me.

Step forward, said the Magistrate with the long iron staff, dressed in great purple robes.

He hid behind wire spectacles, two pieces of glass suspended before his eyes. He occasionally pounded the spiked end of his staff on the floor, sending vibrations through the ground. His robes reflected the fluorescent light blazing around his seated form. He sat in a chair elevated by a flight of stairs. A group of Black Boots stood guard while clerks and stenographers filed documents, shuffled papers, and typed away behind him. They were the people of the fluorescent light, a world of ink and paper. A world filled with the opening and closing of cabinets, files, calendars, and doors. The room was plastered with red flags, all bearing the triangle of three black dots. I loathed the symbol, cared nothing more than to set it aflame.

I did not imagine that this Magistrate was of any importance in the hierarchy of the Democracy. No, I imagined that he was a toady, a yes-man, someone following the orders of his superior. His voice was faint and mousey. He did not strike me as a man of imposing doom, but rather as a servile and ingratiating man. His nasal voice summoned me forward before the court, ever the sound of typewriters clicking their way in the background. It was at best, chaotic. There was no sense of ceremony, but rather a disorderly stream of commands, loose people running to and fro, while the words of the Magistrate struggled to keep afloat amongst the swirling tide of noise.

There were other courts, possibly hundreds, and other Magistrates in purple robes presiding over other guards, clerks, and typists. He was not an important Magistrate, but with his iron staff in hand, he commanded my fate. The tinkling of the anthem played faintly in the background. I stepped forward.

What are the charges brought against this man? He hissed. He did not recognize me. He had skin like a snake, slithery and unctuous. What is the file number? Where did you find this one?

The guard spewed his answer: We found him on the bridge, with some little brat. He is covered in blood, sir. I do not reckon it is his own. The guard stepped back and retrieved some papers from a file, shuffled them in his hands, and gave them to the presiding Magistrate.

What is your name, heathen? The Magistrate looked down at me without recognition. Speak now.

I, I am, I paused.

There is something familiar about you. The Magistrate looked at some papers on his desk, as if he was searching for something. He read a passage quietly to himself. His eyes opened widely and he whispered to the guard beside him. He stood up and suddenly there was a great confusion before me. The figures pointed at me, whispered to each other, the clerks paid attention to the words that the Magistrate hid from me.

Is it him? I overheard the conversation. He read from the paper: Blum, #3 from the 53rd division was released months ago into the desert. He has escaped and is armed and dangerous. Desertion, insurgency, homicide, high treason, his crimes go on. The Golden Council suggests he should be dealt with severely.

The Magistrate raised his staff, and in unison, the clerks behind him stopped their tasks and held their hands up in agreement. They quickly resumed their business.

How should we proceed, your majesty? The Black Boot inquired.

With long drawn out breaths the Magistrate curled out his words. It seemed as if he was exhausted, winded. It was as if my presence had somehow afflicted him with pain. What say you prisoner, how do you plead to these charges? I did not know what to say, and so I did not speak.

Silence prisoner? Is silence your answer, your final plea? He paused and I did not respond. Silence begets more silence. You are a fool. He did not smile. Bring him before the High Magistrate, I heard him shout as the Black Boots clasped my shoulders. His iron staff banged on the floor.

The scene looked familiar. It was an octagonal room with a balcony that overlooked the level where I stood. At its far end sat the High Magistrate's massive golden throne. The faces did not remove their eyes from me. It seemed like a dream that I had lived before, something I had experienced long ago.

You have come to us again, the High Magistrate spoke from his throne. He exhaled large puffs of white smoke from his bruise-colored lips. Speak, tell me how you enjoyed the time you spent in the desert?

He laughed and the audience of golden masks followed his lead. Do you know what your fate will be, Blum? The High Magistrate inquired from behind his gold mask. I looked at him but did not respond. The man came forward from his seat, into the light of the room.

He removed his mask. I looked into his face composed of worms and old earth, he was practically dead, an ancient man, the one I had failed to kill years before, the one who should have received the knife instead of my sweet Isabelle. Here he is, the man I will kill, I thought to myself. He stepped closer and closer to me.

Blum, for most these luxuries are suspended. It is important for you to note that I have not killed you on the spot. I can assure you that you will die one day. There was silence as he walked around me. Look at you now, pathetic. There is nothing I despise more than one who thinks himself better than I, better than God himself.

There was a cheer from the crowd.

Look at you now, nothing more than a serpent slithering on the floor. Your father is dead, Blum. He served us well, as you will now.

He was not my father, I screamed.

Quiet, he shouted as he lashed out and scratched my face with his blade-like nails. The Black Boots held me down on the floor. You are his son, a broken part of his line, and a bastard to that whore. Nothing goes unnoticed in my metropolis, this city of God. He smirked at me. You have enjoyed whores yourself, have you not Blum?

Yes, I am indebted to your father for his contributions to the Democracy. Though, his vices got the better part of him in the end, would you not agree? His boots pounded on the stone floor. My thoughts of you have changed as of late. There are similarities between you and your father that I admire. He paused and tilted his head. In your, shall we say, spirit. It will be in his honor that you, Blum, shall become what you despise most.

My hands tried to break free of the straps, but I was not strong enough to tear them. All heed, the machine that is broken must be melted, molded anew. He turned away from me and walked back to his throne. He stopped momentarily and turned his head to the side so it was in profile. Before the end of this year you will be broken, Blum. You will be rendered anew. The man in the flowing robes sat down on his throne. You will become an Overman, something your father would have been quite pleased with, instead of the bastard that you are. He cackled, as did the others in the crowd.

What have you done with Asha? If she is hurt, you will suffer for it.

The child is as good as dead, Blum.

I'll kill you, I screamed.

She should have died years ago, but your father did not have the heart to kill her.

So Asha is my child, I exclaimed.

He continued: I suppose he was too weak.

I looked at the Magistrate before me as he cast a hateful gaze in my direction. I saw beads of sweat trickling down his oily nose.

Before long you will not even remember your precious brood or the whore that birthed her. I do remember how your father took such pleasure in cutting her so. He sliced at the air with an imaginary knife and smiled widely.

I did remember her: her waving hair, the screams of passion as I entered her, her green fluorescent gaze. My Isabelle, I remembered her all too well. No trauma could free me from her enchanting memory.

What a blind fool you are, Blum. The High Magistrate chuckled.

I stared at him. From the depths of my soul I released the words, both firm and free, they floated upwards to the heavens, past the smoke and the birds, towards that great ball of flame. The words flowed from my heart, a heart that Isabelle would have found irresistible.

I screamed: You, it is you, not I, who are the blind fool.

From a savage rage, the last act of a dying man, an act born of revenge, I broke my leather bonds and launched myself at the Magistrate to inflict my final retribution before the darkness. My claws flung through the air and I jumped on top of him. The Black Boots raised their guns. I tore wildly at the old man's robes, not the robes of God, just a man. I bit hard into the neck of that foul tasting bureaucrat. I was no greater than a common beast, but he, he was even less. His blood infused with my own as I gorged on his neck.

I felt the bullet pierce my back, felt myself bleeding, screaming, being dragged away. The sound of the alarm rang throughout the complex.

Take him away, the High Magistrate screamed through bloody gasps.

I felt their firm hands clutch my shoulders as they carried me spilling out in every direction down the corridor. I licked my bloodied lips and savored each and every drop of revenge. As I was dragged along the floor, past the flags and the Black Boots, I heard the sound of underground trains reverberating through the ground.

VIII

I woke up in a small room covered in a set of padded tiles.

Where am I? I said.

The floor was made of linoleum, easy to clean puke, piss, and shit off of.

Where am I? I said, as if the emptiness had not heard me.

There were no windows. The bed I sat on was small, bolted to the floor. There was a white door in front of me.

How long have I been here? I asked the white walls.

I listened closely to the sound of the buzzing white lights.

Thoughts poured through me: Isabelle, the desert, Jex, my father, Asha. Where is Asha? My body was covered in gauze. The wounds on my torso had been stitched up. Thoughts came and went, bled through me, out of me, and then were forgotten. Some memories stayed for a minute and then flew out of the room. My thoughts vanished completely with the coming of the numb smell.

The room reeked of anesthetic, of ether. They pumped it in through the vents. I hated the smell; it was thick, like the cotton gauze covering my wounds. It made the inside of my nose swell. It made my throat numb. The smell was so dense it filled the room, had replaced the oxygen around me. I was like a bird left too long under a glass jar. Even though I fluttered about the room, batted my wings up at the tiles on the walls, pulled on the door, nothing gave, nothing could set me free.

I knew they were watching me. They saw and charted my every move. I had become a subject for their education. I was the vehicle for their ideologies, their cognition, their foresight, their theory, theorem, and thought. As the High Magistrate had said, it was I who was to become an Overman, the embodiment of the future of the Democracy itself.

I sat there and watched the door. I counted the tiles on the walls. I could not feel my body. I pinched my arm, scratched my hands, pulled my hair out; I couldn't feel it. I paced the small confines of the room. I stepped exactly in the center of each square tile, and counted them as I circled the room. I walked in diagonal patterns, diamond shapes, rectangles, formed strange polygons around my bed, time and time again.

I didn't hear her come in. Long pointed nails poked gently into the flesh of my lower back. I was startled, yet too sedated to react. She leaned over me in her little white coat. The name Morgan was stitched onto the crisp white. She bowed herself over me: white face, red lips, sulfurous brown eyes. She poked the needle into my arm and drew the sample of blood. I saw red flecks inside her eyes, they were reflections of her garish red lipstick. I couldn't help but look at her thighs, her calves, the way her hair was bound up in a long ponytail. I couldn't help but notice the shoes she wore, white pumps with a thick heel.

I savored each second her full form spread across me. She inadvertently pressed her breasts to my chest as she reached across my body. She took my hand, cut my nails, and taped my fingers together. She bound my hands with two small white gloves. They had no finger slots, mittens. I could not pull my hair out.

I imagined her as Isabelle. I loved her smell, reveled in the feeling of her soft hair, delighted in seeing her ruby lips. If only for a moment, a brief moment of interaction, my senses craved her body, her smile, her small fingers touching my skin, her nails on my back. Everything about the nurse excited me, though she was just a distraction from my thoughts of Isabelle.

It's time for your medication, she said in a serious tone. I sat up in place.

What time is it? Where is Asha? Where am I? I asked her.

She did not respond. She walked over to the little cart she had brought into the room and counted out some pills. She returned from the cart with a white tray. On the tray were small piles of pills and a paper cup filled with water. I swallowed the pills, the last was bitter and left me groggier than before.

What time is it, I repeated.

It is half past ten in the morning. You have been asleep for weeks, Mr. X.

Mr. X? I whispered.

She did not respond, instead she smiled at me. Her smile stimulated my desire for her touch. I had forgotten how a woman could move, had forgotten the desire to engage with another body. Though I had forgotten the feeling, the sensation of ejaculation, I knew I desired it with her, the nurse who looked so much like Isabelle.

The child, where is the child?

Are you feeling better today? She parted her lips with a bashful smile, two red slices of watermelon split on a white tablecloth.

Yes, I replied, confused.

My brain was fogged in. My emotions were suppressed by the white pills, the blue pills, the green pills. I felt numb, cold, exhausted, and anesthetized from the gas that continually poured into my room through the vents.

She held out her hand to me with a small white dish. On the dish was a line of soft powder. Take your Offering, it will bring you closer to God, she said. I tried to pull my head away but lacked the strength to do so. I sniffed the Dust into my nose, felt myself overcome with old emotions, felt the energy writhing in my bones. I have failed Isabelle, I thought as I leaned back in the bed.

Okay, Mr. X, I'm going to leave you alone so you can rest. Dr. Barton wants you to be completely rested for today's therapy.

Dr. Barton. Where am I? I thought.

She collected her things and put them on the cart. I watched her figure as she bent over to pull the brake free. Her little white pumps left the room. I closed my eyes and went to sleep.

In dream I saw the dead eyes all around me. Isabelle, Zarian, Jex. I made out the eyes of twins, young boys and girls, staring at me from the corners of my room. I saw the shapes of children, pale eyes, floating eyes, nothing more than specks of energy floating between the space between my bed and the walls. They stayed for a moment and then left. The Midnight Man was watching.

I heard a knock at the door. I got up and moved slowly towards it. It felt as though I was moving through water. I grasped the knob and turned it. I stepped out into the hallway to find that no one was there.

The hall extended for hundreds of feet to the left and to the right. Like a mirage, the corridors rippled and curled in front of me. The ends of the hallways were clouded in dark steam. Doors branched off at various points that led to other rooms, like the one I left behind. The walls undulated as I moved down the hall. The stained wallpaper swirled in loose patterns. Bits of broken glass were scattered on the floor. They turned into liquid beads and then reformed. As I walked on, small fingers pressed through the walls and reached out towards me. Burn marks covered the ceiling, scarred the floor in places. Sheets of peeling and smoldering wood were exposed to the stale air.

I slowly moved down the hall toward the dark area at its end. My heart began to beat faster, small droplets of sweat collected on my scalp and dripped down my forehead. My hands were sticky. When I looked down, I noticed small ripples extending along the floor where my feet touched the ground. The lights in other patients' rooms extinguished as I passed them. I peered in quickly before the darkness consumed them: a set of small children slept in white beds, a woman with wrinkled old skin, a man as white and pale as a ghost.

One of the lights did not go out. I stopped to look inside. A woman sat on the corner of her bed facing away from me. Her nails were painted bright red. Her light brown hair flowed down her breasts, two rolling hills emerging out of fields of golden wheat. She looked beautiful, even more beautiful than Morgan. Another body, much smaller, slept in the bed. I looked closer and saw that it was Asha.

Isabelle? I whispered. The words took the form of smoke and sank to the floor in small puddles.

My breath fogged the observation glass as I continued to watch her.

She was unaware that I observed how she moved her hand along the sleeping child's back. Her hair looked like it was suspended underwater. It moved irrespective of gravity. Each strand reached towards the ceiling, billowed in the currents of air. She turned to face me.

She was my Isabelle, and yet she was not. She seemed hollow and vacant. Her form wavered between a transparent and opaque state. She turned to look at me. I stared into her eyes, painted the color of green sea-glass. The lights in the room went out.

I moved toward the end of the hall, until I could no longer see. When my eyes adjusted to the darkness, I made out the shape of a body hiding in the shadows. I crept along, buried myself in the darkness as much as possible to try and get closer to the shape. I stopped and looked as sharply as I could at the silhouette that moved slowly back and forth before me.

Hello, I whispered into the black. No response.

I wore the darkness like a great velvet cloak. It hid my pallid skin, my shaking limbs, my white teeth chattering inside my skull box. I stepped closer, fearing the Midnight Man had come to haunt me. I heard faint breathing. I felt a chill breath slide along the hair that dusted my arms and face. I could not see the form that stood beside me. I could not control my trembling legs. I was certain the figure before me could feel the vibrations rippling through the ground.

Blum, Isabelle's small voice whispered to me from the shadow.

Her voice seemed distant, though I knew that she was close by. I breathed a sigh of relief. Isabelle stood only a matter of inches from me. I knew that if I extended my arm I could touch her cold skin, her tousled hair, her slender body. I knew I would once again discover a

208

delicate young woman in the prime of her youth.

Can I touch you, Isabelle? I said.

No. Her voice was weak. You dare not touch one who has touched death. I wanted so badly to reach out and touch her but I refrained. I was so anesthetized that the joy I felt was almost entirely suppressed by the drugs.

Blum, this place is evil. She sighed. They will break you. Your patricide has brought you closer to his hands. It is only a matter of time before the end. The Midnight Man watches us, even now. I felt the cold surround my body. I am lost Blum, alone, lost in the smoke. I despair that you will not be able to set me free.

I will free you from his evil grasp. I will. I will free Asha, and I will free you. The High Magistrate has not yet won. My words puffed out in front of me and, like the others, collected at my feet.

Blum, the Midnight Man holds me here until my murder is avenged. He knows something that neither you nor I could possibly know. He has knowledge of your fate that we lack. There is a choice before you Blum, and I fear that you will lose your soul to him. He has planned it that way. He has chosen you because he knows the choice you must make. I fear that the two of us will wander lost inside the fire forever. We will never be together again.

Isabelle, there is no temptation that could take me off my course. I swear to you. I know the choice before me. I would never hurt Asha. I would never commit the infanticide he calls for. He will not have his way in this matter.

Do not rule out the possibility that he sees something that we do not. I fear him, as you should. He passes through the shadows of your room, the dim places, when the lights of the world above you are out. She breathed a raspy breath. He will come for you soon, the hour of your contract will soon expire. Yet, he will wait in the shadows until the choice is upon you, until you fall, and then he will take you to your damnation.

I love you, Isabelle.

There is little time, Blum. Do not give the Midnight Man what he desires.

Isabelle, I cannot bear to have you suffer.

She was gone. I felt helpless. Anger boiled inside of me.

Isabelle and Asha, I must free them, I said to the darkness.

⊙

I awoke to the bite of Morgan's whip digging into the soft flesh of my back. One, two, three, the cat of nine tails scratched me. It opened up long, deep troughs in my skin. The anesthesia, the smell of ether floated heavily in the room. The sensation of her flailing me, time and time again, left me pathetic and cringing. When my thoughts drifted to what lay underneath her black leather skirt, when I imagined her sex, she whipped me harder. I looked at her mouth, it glistened with saliva, her hair was coated in sweat from the red-hot lights. She wore dark black makeup that covered her eyes in a solid band. She looked beautiful, a crimson angel wrapped in a coat of tar. She wore scant leather garments and oversized boots. Her breasts were exposed to the hot lights.

Mr. X, I will break your desire for the flesh, Morgan screamed into the room. First the flesh, then the mind, and lastly the spirit. You will become what we desire you to become. You were once our prisoner in body, and now you will become our slave in mind.

She tightened the chain around my neck. If she had held the chain too tightly I would have passed out of the little white room and into the great unknown of death. I had been stripped naked with my arms and legs spread apart. They were wrapped in chains, which were attached to the tiled walls. Perspiration rolled down my chest and belly, gently graced the divot between my torso and my right thigh, and dripped off of the end of my sex. A puddle of sweat and blood, streaming off of me in small rivulets, collected on the floor below like an unholy offering.

Save me, I screamed as her pace quickened. Stop, I gasped.

You will be saved, she replied. God will save you when you are ready. The sound of her voice echoed powerfully in the red room.

Four, five, six, the cat tails delivered their licks. The soft leather studded with metal brackets tore at me. Striations covered my back. Tears leaked out of my eyes and cascaded over my bruised lips. I bit down on them so I could bear the rapture of her movements. I felt like Isabelle must have felt when my father's knife cut into her. Another blow landed and I let out a shrill scream, something coughed up from deep in my belly, something wild. I spoke the words of languages long dead, long retired, the guttural sounds of primitive men as they murdered each other and ate the flesh of their brethren. Morgan's leather skirt crackled as she danced around the room. Her boots clopped on the linoleum floor. She stopped and began to clean the gore off of her weapon with a bottle of saline solution from the metal tray.

I heard him. Morgan is quite magnificent indeed. Do you agree, Blum? The Midnight Man spoke to me from the shadows, as she continued to clean and polish her multipronged whip.

You are a demon, I hissed.

I know she has visited you, your Isabelle, your love. There is something that I will show you about your beautiful Isabelle, Blum.

The Midnight Man placed his long cold fingers over my eyes, and it became clear to me what he meant. I saw Isabelle inside a column of licking flames. She was caught in the ropes of fire as they blistered her skin and burned her bones. I wanted to reach out and grab her, but I could not move.

Tell me Blum, do you desire revenge for what has happened to Isabelle?

I do not trust you, demon. Isabelle has warned me not to believe anything that you tell me.

The girl wants to protect you, Blum. She would never let you know how much she is suffering. Though, it is she that needs protection, would you not say so, Blum? He laughed as the vision faded.

Leave me be, demon.

Morgan walked over again to continue her sadistic task.

Tell me your fantasy, she whispered in my ear.

I did not know whether to talk or to be silent. To let her know what the dark had uttered to me in my delirium or to express my deep desire for Isabelle. In the moment I desired to be away from my torturer, who hid under black leather and heavy black boots. I remained silent.

Tell me what your fantasy is, pig, she repeated gruffly.

I felt her breasts rub against my exposed jagged skin. Her hard nipples moved from side to side over my wounds. I smelled her sweet perfume, the scent of jasmine, thick, and noxious. My body was entirely hers to use. I did not speak, rather I hoped that she would somehow intuit what I was thinking. I wished that somehow she would know it was time for me to be pardoned, that I had been broken. My skin tingled. She spat on my back.

You're a disgusting pig, she said. You're absolutely swine-like. Then she laughed a little schoolgirl's laugh.

She picked up the whip again. Seven, eight, nine, cats feasted upon my spine. Each thrash, each laceration carved into me. Each tear created tattoos on my back. Each wound festered under the hot lights. I was a martyr, and I knew somehow the pain would give me strength. I took each lashing, each stroke of her spiked flail with an erotic shutter. I was dizzy from her scent, and drunk from the red liquid that poured down me and splashed onto the floor. The blood pooled and then drained through a small hole in the center of the room. The hole connected to the sewers, which ran to the sea. My blood swam freely in the ocean, while my body remained bound. Another blow landed on my broken body.

White dots whirled in front of my eyes. Hot red spotlights focused on my shaking limbs. I felt her whipping me. There was no pleasure in the submission or the power she exuded over me. She made me sweat, made me scream, I was hers.

You're a fucking pig, she shouted.

She pulled my hair fiercely as she continued her forward march into my body. She owned my corpse-like form. I was no longer in control. Her final thrust came heavy upon my fragile bones. It sent a torrent of pain through my shivering, seizing body, and then I passed out. She had caressed every part of my body with her whip. She had used me and enjoyed me as no one had before. She had loved every volatile crack, every scorching sting. My teeth were coated in red wine blood. I had been broken.

IX

I awoke in the white room with Morgan standing over me. My body ached everywhere and I could hardly move. Could this unassuming woman, the one with a light smile and a lovely girl's face, really have been the same who tortured me? I did not want to believe that her angelic breasts were the same ones that had touched the contours of my wounds. No, it cannot be, I thought. She finished feeding me more pills. She forced the Offering into my nose.

The doctor will be with you shortly, she said before the door shut behind her.

It all seemed like a dream. What about the Midnight Man and Isabelle? Had I imagined them coming to me in a nightmare? I felt my back; it was patched with gauze. The wounds did not run as deeply as I had remembered. Long scratches ran down my back. I imagined red fingernails dragging their way across my skin from my neck down to the base of my spine. It felt as though a cat had clawed my back, hundreds of pinpricks and vertical scratches.

A man wearing a white lab-coat entered the room. The name Dr. Barton was stitched onto the breast pocket of his coat. He smiled and drew closer. I was too weak to move. I cringed. He offered me a piece of sugary candy from his palm. I took it and placed it in my mouth.

The candy was chewy and stuck to my teeth. I enjoyed it very much. His hand was sweaty. His appearance was rather unremarkable, except for the circular wire glasses that he wore. He was no older than fifty. A mole graced the side of his neck. It was not a repulsive growth, but rather delicate. It contrasted with the pale white of his laboratory-sheltered skin.

Do you know why you are here, Mr. X? He asked.

Yes, I am your victim. I did not smile.

No, you are quite mistaken. I am here to help you.

He smiled, his eyes dilated as he spoke. His teeth resembled small shells drilled into soft gum.

What if I told you that you could be healthy once again? That you could experience the world, have purpose, meaning, belong to something greater than just yourself. He came and sat on the bed next to me.

He stroked my right leg sensually. The pain was so severe that I could not move. I did not stop him, though I wanted to.

I will let you experience life on a different level, Mr. X. What do you think?

Your words are poison; the Magistrates are poisonous. There is nothing you can do or say to convince me otherwise.

Mr. X, in time you will learn to love the ones who have brought us deliverance. There is a lot of work to be done. There are more therapies we must perform before it is time for you to leave us.

He smiled again. My stomach ached and my intestines twisted. Is it the medication or his words? I thought.

Your father taught me much.

You knew that deranged man? I questioned.

Deranged? Where is your respect? He was a great man, a pioneer. He paved the way for what you will become.

You would make me a monster, I screamed. I thought of the Midnight Man. Both my body and soul were undergoing metamorphoses. I was being changed against my will into a macabre being.

I do not intend to make you a monster. He smiled. I felt my ears fill with sweet sticky nectar, as if he was trying to sweeten my brain before its removal. I'm going to administer some simple tests before today's therapy.

I did not respond, but instead I looked at him with a sullen glare. He riffled through his black bag. He removed a stethoscope and listened to my heartbeat. It beat slowly, methodically. It had been conditioned by the various medications, the Blockers, not to respond to stress, not to pump any harder than it had to. I wondered, as he listened to my heart, what his sounded like. Did his heart beat rapidly? Was he exhilarated by my presence, my captivity? Was he excited by his specimen? Was his heart tender, did he feel empathy for my state, compassion for my distress? I thought not.

Had Isabelle's heart sounded the same before her death? Is this what my father had done to her? Dr. Barton put the stethoscope away and scribbled some notes. He took out a small hammer to test my reflexes. He took my blood pressure. He looked at the inside of my mouth and felt my glands.

You are a fine man, Mr. X. You are strong, adaptable, he stated with enthusiasm. He had me stand up and examined my body both clothed and naked. He remarked at the scratches on my back, but made no notation of them on his pad. He did it all with enthusiasm.

The pungent odor of lemongrass, lavender, and lime wafted up from his collar as he circled me.

He collected samples of my blood, my urine, my stool, my saliva, and my sweat. I felt blatantly exposed, as if he had seen every crevasse of my body. He saw it all, from my eyebrows to the small spaces between my toes. He, in the span of an hour, had seen me go through birth, puberty, and adulthood. Would he see me reach my death as well?

I felt the Midnight Man's eyes from the corners of the small white room. I felt the presence of death beside me. I wanted to cry, and when the tears did start to pour down my face, amidst my sighs and deep exhalations, he exclaimed: Yes, Mr. X., fantastic. Just like that, a few more and my vial will be full. He grinned at me. He could not recognize my tears as such, could not perceive the emotions that, though deadened by the anesthetic, emptied out of me, flowed over the top of his vial, and poured out onto the linoleum floor.

Shortly after, he was finished.

Good day, Mr. X. I will see you at your appointment later today. Until then, try to rest. The nurse will get you when the therapies are prepared. I will see you later.

Loneliness and desperation made me recall Isabelle's tortured body. I felt nothing but pain. I wanted so badly to see the High Magistrate dead, and to believe that I could set Isabelle free. The white pill made me groggy again.

☉

My head was inside a box. The inside of the box was covered in mirrors. I did not understand the technology. I looked forward into my reflection and saw the image of myself reflected unendingly upon itself. My head ran miles and miles, in all directions, at the same time. It felt as though my skull was at the nexus of X, Y, and Z, the absolute center of the universe, the middle of both time and space.

I had momentarily forgotten about my body, the torso that was attached at the base of my neck. I could not even feel my body. It felt like it was suspended, floating in a pool of water. I wondered if they were going to drown me? The anesthetic and the pills had created a division within my own body. The part high above enjoyed the magnitude of self-reflection, while the one below I could not feel or move.

As I waited for the doctor's experiment to begin, the faint tune of the anthem filled my ears. It began slowly and then it became faster. Layers of voices, then strings, and horns, followed by deep percussion, built upon one another. With a crescendo, the anthem shook the box. It vibrated my eardrums. My pulse kept time with the raging music. Each cell filling my boney skull resonated to the tune of the song, a song filled with pride, bravado, and a sense of dignity. At first I resisted its force, but each time I pushed it away, it seemed to grow stronger. With each breath, the force of it filled me. I thought that the melody, as infectious as a child's rhyme, would resound inside my head for an eternity.

The torment did not come from the volume, but rather the repetition. The cyclical nature of the verses caused them to fold in on themselves and then repeat. There seemed to be no end to it. The beginning and the end were both one and the same. I could not separate the movements; they flowed from one to the next so fluidly, so quickly, so incredibly that I could not discern a single note but rather a gathering of notes, a coven of sounds. The long, melodramatic, and glorified sound of tambourines, cellos, and horns ricocheted from glass to glass.

Cacophonous as it was, I began to hum the tune to myself. The hours passed. It must have been hours, and though I did not feel bored it was terribly uncomfortable. As time slid along the glass mirrors that told the tale of my face one million times, I began to sing. The words came quietly at first, but as the minutes passed I felt impassioned; I embellished the tune with my own twists and turns, came up with clever harmonies, logical counterpoints, and even deep and echoing bass tones that I did not know my vocal cords were capable of. Before I knew it I was screaming the song, shrieking it at the top of my lungs, and my smile was almost so wide that it filled the box, millions of teeth, like stars, spread across the glass, across the universe in which I was the very center, the very point of exaltedness, a deity in a land fashioned from glass. My reflection hummed the nationalist tune as my head rocked gently to the side and exhaustion took me to sleep.

☻

I awoke in bed, the Doctor took more of my blood, and then proceeded to ask me some questions:

If there were a God, what would God be?

I did not know the answer and was at a loss for words.

Take your time, Mr. X.

I recalled the sounds inside the box, the happiness that it had provided me compared to the boredom, the sterility, the whiteness of my small room.

I spoke quietly: The music, or rather the creator of that beautiful music. He wrote down my response. A pause. I felt like I was with God inside that box.

Why do you think God created the music for you to hear? Another pause.

God wants me to be happy. I smiled a little bit, remembered the flowing notes that blended inside my ears. Again he wrote the results down.

Where is God, Mr. X?

In the box, I answered.

The words came out of me like they were pulled out by a fishhook. It shocked me how I had answered so quickly, without thought or hesitation. Yet, as I heard myself utter the words, I felt content with their arrangement, their placement, and stood by them with pride.

Are you God, Mr. X?

No. I paused as the thought saddened me, left me feeling even more alone. I am not God. I cannot be God. I do not know the way to salvation.

What if I told you that there were some that helped God create the music, helped deliver the music to us.

Almost automatically I responded: Then they would be amongst those with God, Dr. Barton.

Very good, Mr. X. That is all for today.

Morgan came in the room. I did not think much more about the questions he had asked, but rather stared at her. I was afraid of her slightest movements.

Nurse prepare the next therapy, the doctor said nodding at her.

Yes Doctor, she answered him as she delicately licked her lips, an unconscious movement, something automatic. But to me, as she coated them in slick, wet saliva, I could not help but shiver in fear of her.

I wondered if I would ever hear the intoxicating sounds that had filled me with God's presence again? I had been practically spilling over with God. I remembered the blissful sounds, chanted them time and time again. I heard the sounds at all times in my mind. When my mind drifted to think of Asha or Isabelle my thoughts were clouded by the harmony of that glorious tune.

⊙

As the days went on the therapy became more intense. Instead of just a box, I stared at my reflections in a small, mirrored room. It was piled high with white powder, and Dust continually rained from the sky. The golden face of the High Magistrate had been painted on the ceiling. He watched me from above, gifted me with Offering as I sang his praises, sang his anthem. I felt like an angel covered in blinding white flame. I squinted, tried to see what produced the fine white chalk from his golden face, which was wreathed in a halo of green halogen bulbs, but I could not discern its mystical source.

As I covered myself in white bliss, I felt the closeness of God even stronger than I had before. The music blasted while I sang a continuous stream of sharp notes. The space had never been this large. I had room to move and dance around. I was surrounded by mirrored reflections of myself. There had not been such gifts, such divine food to feast upon when only my head was inside the box. It was then that my entire body experienced what my mind had experienced before.

He was bleeding for me, sacrificing of himself, pouring the white powder down upon me for my benefit, my enjoyment, for being his loyal servant. As my heart raced out of control and my eyes twitched, I started to believe that I was at the nexus, where the light beats off of the backs of angels. I laughed out loud as I rolled, covered myself in it. I made angels in the white Dust.

I laughed and screamed: Open your mouth, my golden liege, and feed me.

As I hungrily stuffed heaps of Dust into my mouth, I felt the divinity of his praise. I dragged my raw fingers through it and rolled my body in it. Though my nose bled, I felt God in that sensation, the glorious euphoric numbness induced by those silky particles.

This is divinity, I said aloud, and he is the one that has made it all possible. The bringer of God, I exclaimed.

I glanced at Dr. Barton, who appeared to me as an angel. He watched me from the observation deck and took notes furiously on a small clipboard he carried around.

Good, that's enough. Get him out of there, he said.

The orderlies came to drag me out of the pit of Dust. They wore masks and body suits to protect themselves from the powder. I tried to resist, I clung to the powder, inhaled as much as I could before it was pried from my hands. When they pulled me out, they did not even see the form I had imprinted in the hill, that of an angel, like one a child would have made in frozen snow.

They washed me in the metal basin for hours. My mind spiraled out of control. My limbs shook and felt as though they were crawling with worms. They had removed my wings, my feathers, and doused my celestial fire. Where had the feeling of divinity, the soft powder underfoot gone? They took me to an adjacent room, small and dark, no God to be seen. I waited for hours, days, time stood still. My stomach reeled. My lungs exhaled shallow breaths.

I felt I would certainly die without the Offering. I needed so desperately to feel God again.

Why are you punishing me? I screamed into the dark room. I will do anything for you. I repeated time and time again.

Just as I entertained the thought that perhaps I could burrow through the walls to get back to the hill of Dust, I saw the face of the High Magistrate appear once again on the ceiling. I stared at it and danced about with elation. I honored his noble face, and held my hands up in prayer towards his greatness.

Give me your blood, give me your skin, give me your bones. I howled the words over and over as I fell to my knees.

When my eyes began to tear, the Dust began to rain out from between his lips. It collected under his beautiful form, just for me. By his divine will he granted it for me, and me alone.

Oh you are such a generous creator, I screamed as the Dust fell. I eagerly snorted it.

I felt honored that he had listened to my prayers, that he had once again granted me the sensation of being a God among men. I loved the being that let me bask in his fountain of ash. He was surely God himself, the creature that would make me an angel once again.

The three dots glowing from his face flashed as his visage dimmed. I stared up from the floor, mesmerized. I reeled in the pleasure of the powder. I felt God inside those three orbs. I desired to feel the body of God inside of me.

☺

I was upside-down, hanging, like a caterpillar's cocoon, all twisted, coated in a rich brown lacquer. The oils, the lotions they rubbed onto my naked body, smelled like iodine. They stained my body the deep color of mahogany wood. My rust-colored skin was exposed, and every wrinkle, every pore resembled the fine grain of a burled walnut. The visitors in the room observed me.

My feet were bound with an iron clasp. They were held in place by a metal strut connected to an I-beam. I hung there, neither dead nor alive. All my blood flooded into my downward facing extremities, a down that had once been up. I was falling, and yet static, caught somewhere between up and down. My body followed the Y-axis, acted as part of the structure of the building, an adjoining support beam. Inside I knew if the pressure of the great roof that housed me had been pressed against my nude form, I could have, only for a moment, resisted its fall, held the building like Atlas holds the earth, only for a brief second, before the collapse, before the shattering, before it came down and crushed me, a high heel grinding a cigarette butt into the ground.

The wax and juice of camphor berries covered my sticky form. Morgan had rubbed the oils and solvents into my naked skin. She wore white surgical gloves that had been covered in powder. The gloves made a snapping noise when she pulled them across her red fingernails. I liked the way the latex smoothly maneuvered across my buttocks, my calves, and the soles of my feet. I thought the carapace I wore might encase me forever, that I would never be rid of the stench of pulpy wood and berries.

The room was full with military doctors. I listened to Dr. Barton.

Gentlemen, I assure you that he is the most successful case in my study, my research. He coughed and then lit a cigarette that he breathed in and puffed out in large clouds. It covered me in an acrid odor.

He said: This is by far the subject with the most potential. He has been most responsive to the therapy, is primed. He is ready for the next phase.

The group of men that surrounded him clapped their hands emphatically and smiled. They were small men with gray faces. They were not handsome, but they were not ugly either. Each wore a lapel with the symbol of the Democracy embroidered on it, three black dots forming a triangle. The High Magistrate was not amongst the men below me. I looked closer as one of the men lit a cigarette. The flame flickered, barely caught the end of his stick. The lighter was made of silver. The symbol of the Democracy had been etched onto it.

One of the visitors spoke: The High Magistrate demands results, Dr. Barton. How much more time, how much more energy — the resources you have used, it would be a true waste, a true shame, such a dishonor if you were to fail.

The words he said were deep, they were filled with energy that started very low in his abdomen and rumbled their way out of his throat. When his words left his lips they forked out like spears and landed with gravity in the ears of the men that accompanied him.

Of course, just wait and see. You must observe and then you will understand. The result of the therapy is close at hand, but it takes time.

We don't have time. Time is a luxury of the past, the man yelled.

Yes, on with it then. We don't want to waste any more time.

They have come to see my change, my metamorphosis, I thought. I imagined they wanted to see me transform right then into a butterfly, wanted me to please them with my multicolored wings. If I could have turned myself into that bug, from man to bug, and back again, I would have done so in order to please them.

I should have been afraid, but I was sedated from the pills. The lights turned off, and the screens on the walls lit up. Then the images appeared. They were very small and quiet at first. I began to feel a warming sensation in my toes, then my knees, then my belly, my guts, my heart started to beat slower, my eyesight faded, and the whole world began to spin. The colors on the screen seemed to bleed off of the edges. Although logic told me that it was not real, it felt real, it felt so very real.

The screens surrounding me filled with the symbol of the Magistrates. My ears were full of the music of the Magistrates. My body began to vibrate at the sight of the triad of orbs, as electricity passed through my legs and into my brain. The glyph seized my thoughts, filled me with a delirious euphoria. I did not understand why they had hung me in that position, though I imagined it was of benefit to the science, the experiment, the therapy as the doctor had called it.

The men smoked their cigarettes in long relaxed draws as they watched me. I let my mind relax and knew without any sort of confirmation, other than that precious symbol, that divine notice, that signal from above, that mark of celestial power, that I had been transported through time and space. I prayed that they would send word of my holy sacrifice to the High Magistrate, the very godlike man that mesmerized and hypnotized my mind through the symbol born of civility, justice, and strength.

When they turned up the music, I experienced a raw and primal instinct I had not expected. Never before had I felt so close to the presence of God. The feeling overtook me, overwhelmed me, it felt like an orgasm, a burst, a surge, a kinetic overflowing of pleasure. The anthem rang inside my head and I knew, I knew then, from some natural point inside of myself, that the doctor had been right, I had learned to love the Democracy.

I shook the poisonous thought from my mind.

X

I was exhausted; fatigue melted my muscles. Morgan had wheeled me into a small white room, like the first I had occupied. She laid out my pills on a tray beside my bed and unlatched my restraints. I was able to crawl into bed with her assistance. She smiled at me.

You're doing so well with your progress, Mr. X. You are almost cured.

I was still dazed and intoxicated from the therapy, but drifting through the metal pipes connecting the rooms, I thought I heard the cries of a small child. Her voice was interrupted by gasps for breath.

Do you hear that, Morgan? Where have they taken Asha, I asked her.

Morgan put the pills in my mouth and watched me swallow them. I shook my head to try and clear it. I choked on the cold water as it coated my dry throat. The Dust still coated the inside of my esophagus.

Will I see her again? I asked.

You are just imagining things. It is a byproduct of the therapy. It will pass. You need to rest, Mr. X. You are doing so very well, wouldn't you say? I know you are excited by the progress, but you need to get your rest. She stroked my head and ran her fingers through my hair.

You must help her. I said desperately.

She continued to smile at me. Please sleep, Mr. X.

I must tell you something, Morgan.

What is it, Mr. X? She smiled.

Since being here, I have learned not only to love the Democracy, but you as part of it, and the doctor, and more importantly the Magistrates. That is why you must understand that I say this to you out of love. You must help me find my daughter.

I can do no such thing. Your loyalty will be rewarded by God, Mr. X.

I leaned over so as to embrace her, and she leaned into me. I held her breasts to my chest firmly.

I have so much love for you, Morgan. It is truly a pity.

Still holding me: Why is that? What is a pity?

I put my hands on either side of her face gently, she held onto my forearms like a mother. We exchanged a loving glance, and then I snapped her neck like a rotten fruit from an old gnarled tree. Her body fell to the floor.

I placed her in my bed, pulled the sheets up around her face so it could not be seen. They would discover her soon enough. They would come for me. I needed to find Asha quickly. I removed the pills from under my tongue. I broke them apart and smeared the wet powder onto the sheets.

I must find Asha. I need to know that she is okay.

The door clicked open with the turn of Morgan's key. The hall was quiet and empty. I could not determine where I was, each hall looked the same. Each hall looked so institutional, filled with the scent of stale food and pills. The air gave me an intense feeling of nausea. I remembered my dream and walked towards Asha's room.

As I walked down the halls my skin began to itch. I scratched myself in places along my neck and around my ears. In some places I scratched so hard that I ripped open raw holes in my dry skin. I felt the need for the Offering. I understood that the longer I went without it, the more desperate my actions would become. I needed to find her.

I quickened my pace, almost running down the hall under the broken lights. Fluorescent tubes spanned the ceiling. Some were missing in places, cracked, or broken. Some flashed on and off. My heart pumped loudly. I frantically searched for Asha's room. In that moment, in the very crux of deliberation, my heart pounding, jumping, leaping, an uncontrollable arrhythmia of reaction, I wanted the comfort of the Dust so badly.

Asha sat on her bed crying. She did not notice me. I tried two keys before finding the one that opened her room. The hall was still silent. As my hands twisted the knob to open the door, the voice spoke to me.

You are going to die, Mr. X, Dr. Barton said ominously over the loud speaker. Both you and the girl will die should you not go back to your room willingly. Dr. Barton spoke with finality in his voice, he spoke in doctrine and decree, he spoke in law.

I felt the reaction begin in my toes. They started to tingle. Then my knees began to tremble, my stomach tightened, and my chest felt tight. My legs unconsciously began the march back to my room.

My body responded automatically, compulsorily. There was no thought involved, no command from my cortex. Quite contrarily, my legs began moving before I even realized in my mind that they had started to move. I walked steadily back down the hall towards my room. I desired the great face of the High Magistrate and the Offering that poured from his mouth. I desired the stimulating sensation of being entirely aware, no longer dreaming, full of enlightenment, full to the top with God and his wonderful electricity. I desired to be filled with the glorious sensations the Dust offered. There will be no death, no Midnight Man, there will be nothing but ecstasy, I thought. I was returning to the doctor and his white gloves.

The anthem began, and as I marched along I lost myself in song and movement. I belted the words from my brain, not my heart. I moved in step with the beat of the percussion instruments, and I sang the high melodies of the strings. I unconsciously smiled, lips pulled apart by the sweet symphony. I hailed the Magistrates, and even the doctors for their work, their contributions. My words and actions were mechanical. I did not know the words that I uttered, and still I spoke them to the bright lights, sang them to an audience of white tiles that held me up as I led the band forward.

Death, there will be no death for me, I said.

Through the anthem I heard Dr. Barton. Very good,

Mr. X. I knew you would come back to us. I knew that you could not leave us, your family, so easily.

The word *family* lingered in my ears. I remembered Asha. I had opened her room. I had begun to do something, and yet could not remember what. I was overcome with a need for the powder.

They grabbed me before I even realized they were there. Two order-lies wrapped my arms from elbow to fingers in sticky tape and attached them to the chair. They bound my legs, and still I sang the song. I kept my smile, I kept it large and proud, I was somewhere else. I thought of the millions of soldiers fighting overseas. I thought of the battalions of faceless helmets and cheap waving flags. I thought of the tanks and the bombs, and the guns, the fires of liberation, and the strength of the Magistrates' protection.

As they wheeled me away, I could not move my limbs, but I screamed for triumph over the west, screamed for salvation brought by those who stood at the feet of God. I screamed for those who spoke his divine words, the bringers of the Dust, of the great machines, the science, and most importantly the grand purification, the deliberate cleansing and sanitization of independent thought, action, and will. As the lights of the hall moved by me, I cried gems of clear liquid glass. They pushed the chair rapidly down the long hall.

Dr. Barton spoke: Behind this door lies the answer to your salvation, to your purification. You will see the solution and the cure to your affliction. Even death itself will no longer be able to control you. Don't you want to taste and eat of God?

My mouth salivated and I slobbered while I sang. Long strands of spittle issued out of the corners of my mouth, but still I sang.

The orderlies spun me around, burst the white double doors open, and righted me again. The surgery room was quite large, covered from floor to ceiling in mirrors. A second level had been constructed so observers could peer down and watch the doctor's operations. Seated in a large golden throne on the observation deck, the High Magistrate looked at me with squinted eyes. The High Magistrate's neck was bound with thick gauze and bandages, covering the spot where I had permanently left my mark. He was surrounded by dozens of gold masks. The Council had come to watch my birth.

Asha was already inside the room. She was bound up in the same way I was. Her face was pale in the bright lights. She had dark black rings under her sparkling green eyes. Dr. Barton stepped over to me and put his palms on my face. I smelled the Dust on him. When he approached me my desire for it increased, my breathing quickened, the excitement, like a rising orgasm, overtook me.

He let me breathe in the powder, the crushed white pills through nose and throat. He let me lick and gum the fine crystalline particles that remained. At that moment I loved him so much, loved him like a son would love a father, loved him more than I could ever remember loving Isabelle or the child that sank in her chair behind him. I loved him more and more with each splendid inhalation.

Do you want to be saved? The High Magistrate called down to me.

The others wheeled Asha into position. I looked at the High Magistrate, noticed how his brows hung far over his shadowed eyes. His nose hooked out. It created a dark column of shade along the right side of his face. Between his lips, his teeth shone like thousands of diamonds reflecting in the morning sun. His laughter reminded me so much of the Midnight Man's.

Yes, I said quietly, with eyes open wide, eyes that took in all of his grandeur. Then louder: Yes, I screamed.

I felt powerless; I had succumbed to the command of the doctor and his therapy. They hooked me into a chair facing Asha. I felt the prick of needles enter my body. I felt bags being hooked up to my extremities. I felt Dr. Barton clawing at me.

The High Magistrate spoke: With transcendence there comes a price, Mr. X. I could not move; I was strapped into the chair. There is always sacrifice in order to attain greatness, and in your case the sacrifice is blood. I couldn't speak. They shoved a gag-ball in my mouth, and tied its cords securely behind my head.

There will be a new world when we are finished. You will be locked in servitude to the Magistrates. You will be like a vassal to his lord. You will depend on us for command, for life, for God.

Meanwhile the doctor shined his various instruments, scalpels, forceps, and clamps with a white rag.

You will remember that we, he opened his arms to the Council, are the glorious keepers of the word of God. God will have his vassals cleanse the world for the coming of the new sun. From her sacrifice you will be reborn. He laughed a string of deep laughter.

I am ready, I thought, biting down into the rubber in anticipation.

This is part of the grand solution, Mr. X. Consider us all harbingers of a new age. Let it begin.

XI

It felt like a dream. I could not discern what was reality and what was not. In the room there were mirrors everywhere. I distinctly remember the mirrors because they were so bright, illuminated from all sides by the lights hiding in the corners. Asha was there too. Our reflections scattered across an eternity of space, in the octagonal room that was covered from base to apex, from floor to ceiling, in bright white mirrors. We both wore white straight jackets that billowed out at the arms. Our legs were held in place by white leather boots connected to the floor.

Dr. Barton's voice came over the speaker: We will reorder your state, it will be critical to your healing, your process, to the affirmation of your sense of self, memory, time, place. Try to remain calm, try to avoid hysteria, we are only trying to help you, to cure you.

When the speaker turned off, the walls of the room began to rotate, and the images, the reflections, the refractions of our doubles, reflections of our brothers and sisters, our twins spun about us, we being the center of X, Y, and Z.

The lights dimmed. Asha was in front of me. A white rubber gag ball had been jammed into her mouth. It was held in place by cords that circled her head and neck. The cords reminded me of white vines, creeping, growing, twisting on our skulls, which housed the organic matter, the gray tissue, the wrinkled bits of flesh the doctor wanted so badly to renew, revitalize, restore, in his words, purify.

The music started up quite rapidly, not like it had been inside the box, not how it had been pleasantly pumped into the chamber, so entertaining, so amusing. The anthem came through a hidden gramophone locked inside the walls, perhaps inside the control room with Dr. Barton. The jingling tune was underlined with the beat of heavy drums. The sound exploded into the room. It was violent, not pleasing at all. I had such fond memories of my time spent so far away inside the box. It had seemed like a place where only God and I existed.

This new intensity, this new volume, was painful, triumphantly commanding, it was strong, made me fearful of the coming moments. My ears swelled with the music and I cringed, bit down on the rubber gag to relieve some of the pressure that was building in my ears. I could barely see Asha through our spinning reflections, through the waves of noise. A cacophony of absolutism poured through the jarring notes, no longer sweet, no longer melodic, but utterly controlling.

Hours passed, and still the sounds would not relent. After more time, the pain subsided and the melody went to work. I felt areas of my brain filling up with sound, filling up and growing, expanding. I felt other parts turning into liquid, reorganizing, and then solidifying.

When the great face came down from the ceiling, glowing orbs tattooed onto his golden visage, my heart leapt. It was God, formed of pure gold. I prayed that he would save Asha and me. I called out to him to free me from my bonds. I desired to walk free in the grasses, feel the wheat under my fingers, watch birds ride the hot thermals that take them high into the air. I screamed inside my mind. He did not stop the music, and my heart sank into pitiful desperation. I knew he had heard me, I did not know what it would take to receive his divine grace. I revered his face, so knowledgeable, so divine.

The High Magistrate's voice played over the loudspeaker: You please me; therefore, I will deliver you. You please me; therefore, I will reward you. Your existence, your healing, your communion with God relies on my grace; therefore, you will continue to please me, and I will continue to reward you. You are the militia of the saved; therefore, I am your father.

The mantra was spoken. He repeated it over and over, the words flowed around the room, mixed with the pounding sound of drums, the screeching sound of strings, and the light tinkling sound of cymbals, chimes, and triangles.

I wanted so badly to please him. I wanted to be rewarded, to be allowed to commune with God, to ingest of his body. I wanted the powder of his bones inside my nostrils, and the grindings of his dried, salted, and cured muscles, which draped across his celestial body, to be absorbed by the saliva that lined my gums. I wanted so badly for him to let Asha and me inside his grace. I prayed for his mercy to encompass her. Let her be saved, I thought until my eyes began to tear, until my teeth formed impressions on the soft rubber between my jaws. My hands could no longer strain against the weight of the canvas sleeves that bound me in place.

Hundreds of times, thousands of times I heard the mantra, embraced his grace, embraced the savior inside my fragile mind, my liquid mind, my mind so freshly molded, so new, so malleable. I loved him more than ever before. I desired him so much inside my blood and bones, to taste of him on one side while Asha lapped the sweet milk of his salvation from the other.

His voice returned: It is true that I can bring the rain.

From the ceiling tiny beads started to fall down on us, shining pearls, white capsules started to spill out of the mirrors above, small droplets of rain. He had promised us rain, and he had granted it. I wanted so badly to taste the white rain, to taste the pills that poured freely over our skin. When they landed on the floor they burst into small hills of Dust. The ground was littered in them, the ground was covered in a layer of fine ash. The mirrors created the illusion of white rolling plains. I hungered so badly to roll in the Dust, to lick the floor beneath his feet.

My eyes were wide, and my pupils dilated to the very edges of my irises. I was so high on the grandeur of his salvation, on the possibility that we, Asha and I, would be saved. We were the only ones left to be saved. I hoped that we would not end up as ghosts, like Isabelle or the Midnight Man, who walked the halls and hid inside shadows.

The room began to twist on itself faster and faster. The face, the great golden face with its three glowing orbs, spun along its vertical axis, and everything, light, sound, atom, and breath, blended in that moment, in that pinnacle, gave way to the darkness that engulfed the room. I was so hungry, so hungry for the transcendent feeling of salvation that we were to discover.

Your two fates will be one, I heard the High Magistrate speak as my bonds were unlocked and I stepped out of my restraints.

I held a scalpel in my hand, though had no recollection of picking it up. I advanced on the girl. I knew nothing but what he commanded of me.

You must sacrifice the child for the Democracy, Mr. X. It is your final test. It will complete your therapy.

I drew close to Asha's face. She held her eyes closed tightly. I grasped her head and pulled it backwards exposing her throat. I lifted the scalpel and moved it closer to her pulsating neck. Still the mirrors spun, still his words commanded me onward.

Finish her, finish her, finish her, the speaker repeated time and time again.

Then the Midnight Man's voice filled the room: Take the child, Blum. Do as he says and sacrifice the child.

From behind the blackness of the Midnight Man, I heard Isabelle's spirit screaming from the flames: Save her Blum. Remember your promise. You promised me you would protect her.

Isabelle's face flashed before my eyes as the first drop of Asha's blood hit the spinning room's floor. Though the chemicals pumped inside of me, and the Dust triggered euphoria in my head, the song, the mirrors, the face, and the grand symbol spoke to me through and through, I knew it all then as an illusion. Isabelle's plea woke a rage in me. My soul had not been broken. My love for Isabelle and the small child had kept it alive.

I moved the knife from Asha's neck and instead cut her from her bonds. She fell to the floor. Dr. Barton gasped from the observation deck and rushed down to control me. The mirrored room stopped spinning. Dr. Barton came at me wildly with a scalpel. The Council above went into a panic.

The High Magistrate's words filled the room. Sit down, he boomed. Sit down.

The golden faces disobeyed. They raged about, both panicked and fearful that I had risen from near death before them. He is a demon, they screamed as the chaos continued above. The High Magistrate remained seated in his throne and watched me.

Asha could barely stand on her own. She was sedated by the drugs, the euphoria, and the Dust. A small cut spilled blood down from her throat onto her small chest. The lights in the operating room were flickering.

Dr. Barton waved his scalpel at me. We turned in a circle moving around the room. I tried to keep Asha by my side, but like a wounded dog, she crawled over into the corner of the room.

You will not ruin what I have created, he shouted.

You have created nothing but false promises.

Finish him, the High Magistrate screamed.

You would have been a god. The doctor's voice was harsh.

I saw the flash of the knife as it came toward me. Before the knife landed, before I felt the piercing pain of the knife inside my chest, I jumped to the side crashing into a group of glass chemical bottles that were lined up along the mirrors surrounding the room. As the liquids crashed on the floor they ignited into flame.

Look what you have done. You are a traitor.

Sit down, the High Magistrate screamed at the herd of golden masks.

He tried to maintain order over the flood of bodies beside him, but to no avail.

Finish him, the High Magistrate roared over the commotion of the upper level.

Some Black Boots raised their guns and aimed at me. The High Magistrate raised his hand to give the command to shoot. As his hand fell, the second story balcony erupted in roaring flames. Pieces of ceiling burst explosive gases onto the herds of panicked Magistrates and Black Boots. Some toppled over the balcony. Limbs exploded and bodies were swallowed in flame. A gas line had burst.

The fire thickened as it spread up the walls. I was worried for Asha's safety. The doctor saw me look at the child. She was exhausted, lying next to the mirrored walls. We both dashed for her, but he was able to grab her one second before I could.

One more move and the child will die.

Stop, I screamed at him wildly. I will do what you want.

Put down the scalpel.

I threw the scalpel to the floor.

Much better.

He let go of the child and came toward me at full speed. I cowered into a ball, expecting the force of his blow to slash me in half. I closed my eyes and prepared to accept my death, in hopes that he might spare the child.

Asha screamed, and I opened my eyes to see that she had jumped onto the doctor's back and stuck him in the throat with a long needle. She fell off of him as he fell to the ground. The flames caught on Dr. Barton's clothing and he began to burn.

I rushed over to him, and looked at his writhing body. I bent down to finish him. He grabbed my hand. I sliced his neck open like a piece of meat splayed in two. Blood pulsed from the leaking pipe.

The flames spread quickly across the ceiling. I grabbed Asha's hand. I looked up and saw that the High Magistrate had left the upper deck. He had retreated with his faithless minions. The entire building had caught flame. Chemicals and pipes exploded in the walls. The smoke was billowing up in a massive veil of black. I pushed Asha out of the operating room and into the hallway.

We must hurry Asha, we must find a way out. The two of us coughed heavily. We tried our best to cover our faces.

The building erupted into flames, bursting out from under its foundation. The walls rumbled as we raced through the hallways, pushed past the wreckage and debris. Beams had fallen on Lesser Magistrates and orderlies. The halls were littered with flaming death. I feared that moment would be our last.

As we turned the corner, a body moved out of the darkness and snatched Asha from my grasp. The High Magistrate held the child at knifepoint as he slowly backed down the hallway towards the heart of the fire.

Let go of her, I screamed.

She will die, Blum. It is her fate.

The hallway in front of me had remained unscathed, was not yet subject to the conflagration that spread with every second I deliberated. I could have escaped, but instead I crept closer to the demon that held my child.

The High Magistrate held Asha tightly over a pit that had opened up in the ground. Raging fire burst forth from it, gas lines and pipes fed the flames as they rose into a wall behind the High Magistrate. He looked immense in front of the flaming wall, his robes sizzled in the heat of the encroaching fire.

It is futile to try and stop me, Blum.

Let the girl go, I screamed. I was closing in on them. As I stepped forward he lifted Asha, kicking and screaming, closer to the fire. I stopped.

I have said my goodbyes to this life, Blum, and I am willing to accept death, but not without her. This rat will satisfy my revenge, my desire to make you regret the day you turned against me. I am God.

His words billowed out with the black smoke. The High Magistrate held Asha in his hands as she struggled for breath in the darkening hallway.

The end is upon us. This will end here, today, now.

Let the girl go, I screamed. It is me that you want.

You are right. This is between us, Blum. Come for me, undo me like I know you desire to in the deepest part of your soul. However, if you kill me, she will die as well.

He moved Asha closer to the fire. I felt the heat of the fire from my distance, and I imagined that she would soon catch flame.

The feeling that someone's eyes were watching me, filled me with dread. I felt him there, wet and soggy, waterlogged, slithering upon the skin that covered my back. The Midnight Man stared at me from behind.

His voice filled the hall. I did not need to turn and see his ghostly silhouette.

Blum, your obligation still lingers on my mind. I suggest you put an end to all of this, before it is too late. It is over Blum, for you this can all be over. Isabelle can be free. You will die here and now: patricide, infanticide, suicide, the ashes will cover it all. You will rule as I have ruled, you will be king of all of this.

I stepped forward, the Magistrate did not move, his arms tightened around the child. This will be the end, I thought to myself.

You must die, I screamed into the burning halls as I threw myself towards the High Magistrate.

You are a fool, have always been a fool, and will now die as a fool dies, the High Magistrate screamed as I rushed at him.

Finish him, the Midnight Man echoed the High Magistrate's words as I sped forward.

The laughter of the Midnight Man made the smoke billow closer and closer to me. My eyes were beginning to blacken. I could not breathe the hot air. Behind the High Magistrate I saw Isabelle's spirit struggling for breath inside the flames.

Finish him, Blum, and Isabelle will be free, the Midnight Man howled. I looked at the child and she at me. I was almost upon them. Asha trembled in his arms but did not move her gaze from me. I lifted my finger to my eye, motioned a falling tear as I leapt into the air towards the two of them.

As I did so, Asha kicked the High Magistrate in the groin and jammed her hand into his wounded throat, tearing the bandage from his neck. He winced in pain as her hands pried at his loose flesh. Her other hand flew upwards at his face and ripped out his eye. He dropped her and howled in terror. She rolled safely out of my way.

I threw myself into his old, hanging flesh. Blood burst out of his empty eye socket in a crimson stream that caught flame as the two of us fell into the pit of fire.

I looked back and saw Asha right herself and run towards the hall leading to the outside world. I would not see the child again.

The Midnight Man screamed as my body combusted. I had escaped the fate of his dark bargain. Somehow, perhaps by the love that Asha and I shared, I had escaped the inevitability he had foreseen. She knew, as did I, that I could never hurt her. Though I died, our destiny had been changed. Perhaps Asha would live to carry the banner another day, lead the people into an age unlike the one in which I had lived, I thought.

Isabelle's ghost appeared before me. Waves of hot air moved between us, distorting the image of her burning spirit. I was lost inside of her. I looked at her green eyes reflecting the scorching flames. I wanted to hold her face in my palm once more. Singed and burning we embraced each other, and in that moment, in the heat, in the space between this world and the next, we touched for the first time in many years.

Our lips kissed, red hot, like coals burning over an open flame. Each strand of her hair sucked the fire through itself. I felt the pull of time slowing, turning against itself, as the flames progressed up our legs, over our hips, and onto our torsos. The fire worked its way up to feel the pulse of our jugulars. It reached the tops of our heads, kissed our eyelids, and danced along the ridges of our ears as we transformed, like butterflies birthed from great cocoons.

The smell of jasmine, of gardenias, of lavender, of hyacinth, of fresh cut grass filled the air. Hair burned and fingers melted together as we embraced. There was no pain inside her grasp, even though my skin scorched away and my nails melted. The fat from my bones was covered by serpentine ropes of fire.

It felt as though we were under water, as though our two bodies were becoming one, far beneath the tumult of the waves. I saw pieces of sea-glass blowing around us and mermaids swimming alongside of us in the fire. We were undergoing a sea-change: from man to woman, to bones, coral, and sand. From seaweed and algae into the mouths of small fish. From fish to seal and walruses and sharks. From the decaying body of a beached whale, into the mouths of gulls.

Yes, I knew then, that they would take us far over the land, high above the cities, where the people of the great Democracy of the Magistrates spread themselves far and wide. Where the citizens of the Capital, that great metropolis, walk daily towards trains, factories, and machines, spending their days knocking hammers against hard steel. We were free and we flew high, covered in red flaming feathers, into the air towards the sun.

There is a moment before the end when the world recoils from you. As you approach that moment there is a ripple in the space between you and other living creatures. It was indescribable, transparent, still, and quiet. I felt the ripple of energy diminishing between us. It stretched and frayed, an old cable pulled too taut, small fissures, then it ripped apart as we dove headfirst back into the current.